He put down the phone.

'That was the clinic. An emergency admission. It's a pity you're too tired because we could do with an extra pair of hands.'

Clive was opening the door. She hesitated, but only for a brief moment.

'I think I could force myself to work if you really need me.'

His mouth quivered as he smiled down at Penny. 'That's my girl,' he said quietly.

She shook her head. 'No, you're wrong.'

We hope you'll love the forthcoming new look for medical romances. From next month—bright new covers, bright new name, and, of course, the same great stories with a medical theme, for you to enjoy— all from Love on Call.

THE EDITOR

Dear Reader

This month we offer you Accident and Emergency, Cardiac, Physiotherapy, and a holiday resort in Egypt — how's that for variety? Lynne Collins gives us a hero who is dogged by gossip, Lilian Darcy an older heroine coping with passion for a younger man, Drusilla Douglas a heroine confused by identical twins, and Margaret Barker gives us a pair who had met before. . .

We hope you enjoy learning how they solve their problems!

The Editor

Margaret Barker pursued a variety of interesting careers before she became a full-time author. Besides holding a BA degree in French and linguistics, she is a licentiate of the Royal Academy of Music, a state registered nurse and a qualified teacher. Happily married, she has two sons, a daughter, and an increasing number of grandchildren. She lives with her husband in a sixteenth-century thatched house near the sea.

Recent titles by the same author:

HIGHLAND FLING
ROMANCE IN BALI

RED SEA REUNION

BY
MARGARET BARKER

MILLS & BOON LIMITED
ETON HOUSE   18–24 PARADISE ROAD
RICHMOND   SURREY   TW9 1SR

All the characters in this book have no existence outside the imagination of the Author, and have no relation whatsoever to anyone bearing the same name or names. They are not even distantly inspired by any individual known or unknown to the Author, and all the incidents are pure invention.

All Rights Reserved. The text of this publication or any part thereof may not be reproduced or transmitted in any form or by any means, electronic or mechanical, including photocopying, recording, storage in an information retrieval system, or otherwise, without the written permission of the publisher.

This book is sold subject to the condition that it shall not, by way of trade or otherwise, be lent, resold, hired out or otherwise circulated without the prior consent of the publisher in any form of binding or cover other than that in which it is published and without a similar condition including this condition being imposed on the subsequent purchaser.

First published in Great Britain 1993 by Mills & Boon Limited

© Margaret Barker 1993

Australian copyright 1993 Philippine copyright 1993 This edition 1993

ISBN 0 263 78341 3

Set in 10½ on 12½ pt Linotron Times 03-9309-48222

Typeset in Great Britain by Centracet, Cambridge Made and printed in Great Britain

CHAPTER ONE

PENNY was crossing her fingers, hoping against hope that it wouldn't be him! She couldn't bear the thought of spending three months working with a pompous, unfeeling, callous brute. And it would be so embarrassing, considering their last encounter.

She stared out of the window of the dilapidated taxi at the wide esplanade flanking the Nile. Her driver swerved to avoid a horse-drawn calèche that suddenly emerged in front of them.

What a strange mixture of the old and the new — the ancient calèches with their swarthy drivers sitting up front clasping long leather whips, jockeying for position amid the throng of modern cars, and some not so modern, like the one in which she'd just survived the four-hour journey through the desert from Hurghada airport on the Red Sea.

She leaned back against the seat and looked out across the Nile to the west bank where the golden sun was sinking slowly behind the palm trees. An orange glow suffused the water, cutting a swath of colour that seemed to fall on her, as if the sun god felt she needed a blessing at the end of her long, arduous day.

It was a day that had begun with a cold September dawn at Gatwick airport. Not a pretty sight! But what a fabulous ending this was. She was desperately tired, but the magnificent sunset was reviving her spirits. If only she could be sure that the man she was going to work for wasn't *the* Dr Clive Hamilton who'd made such a fool of her five years ago.

She reasoned that it was unlikely to be the same person. The Clive Hamilton she'd known had gone off to West Africa and had never been heard of again. . .not by her, at any rate, thank goodness!

She opened her bag and took out the instructions she'd been given at Gatwick by the special messenger from the nursing agency. She remembered the initial shock when she'd read the name of the doctor in charge of ICMWT — International Clinics for the Medical Welfare of Tourists. But on the plane she'd reassured herself with the knowledge that she was going to work at a very small clinic on the Red Sea. It was unlikely that even if it was the man she wanted to avoid they would ever meet. He was much too important. . .arrogant. . .conceited. . .

The taxi swerved again and the Egyptian driver swore loudly; at least, Penny thought it sounded as if he was swearing at the crowd of tourists jaywalking across the esplanade in the twilight to their hotel.

Oh, she would be so happy to reach her own hotel! When she'd arrived in Egypt she'd been met at the airport on the Red Sea by a nurse who'd told her that a change of plan necessitated she make the long journey to the main clinic at Luxor. It had been almost the last straw.

'Will I be working for Clive Hamilton?' she'd asked the young Egyptian nurse.

'Yes. Do you know him?' the girl had replied.

'I'm not sure,' Penny had said. 'What does your Dr Hamilton look like?'

The girl had shrugged. 'Don't ask me, Sister. I've never seen him. All I know is he's the medical co-ordinator, the big boss of ICMWT. He hasn't been over to the Red Sea but I've seen his name in our official prospectus and I've heard a lot about him. He's a very important man so I suppose he's too high and mighty to come over and visit us.'

'How old is he?' Penny had asked tentatively.

Again the young nurse had shrugged. 'Oh, very old, I imagine.'

Penny had breathed a sigh of relief and climbed into the waiting taxi that the clinic had laid on for her.

But she'd continued to worry all the way through the desert, as she'd gazed in awe at the wide expanse of sand on either side of the newly metalled road that had recently replaced the ancient track beaten down by generations of camels and horses. For several minutes at a time she'd been able to banish her fears, but now they had returned, magnified a million times over, especially as the dreaded encounter could be imminent.

The taxi was pulling into a small crescent-shaped driveway in front of the large, imposing Nile Hotel. She thanked the driver as he carried her large suitcase from the car.

How many of these Egyptian pounds should she tip him? She grasped a few in her hand, hoping it was enough and yet not too many. She wasn't sure how her new salary was going to pan out.

As she walked towards the foyer of the hotel a small band of Egyptian musicians struck up a haunting tune on the drums and flute. To Penny, the sound seemed like the essence of Egypt as she remembered it from films she'd seen. Ever since childhood she'd been fascinated by this country.

She turned and smiled at the musicians, handing over some of her money to the man who looked as if he was in charge of this cheery band. He removed one hand from the drums he was beating; his smile grew broader as he bowed his head.

'*Shukran, madame, shukran.*'

She knew he was thanking her. *Shukran* was one of the words she'd learned on the plane from her guidebook. But there were so many more she would have to memorise if she were to be able to have a fluent conversation. She was hoping that initially most of her patients would speak some English.

The hotel lobby was crowded with tourists: Japanese, English, German. She might have been back in England apart from the whirling fans above her head and the profusion of tall palms that graced every corner, pillar and alcove.

She was aware that the taxi driver had deposited her luggage with Reception and was waiting beside her for his tip. Apparently, wages were very low in Egypt and *baksheesh* was an important necessity. She handed him some of her notes.

'The doctor is sitting over there,' the driver said as the money disappeared beneath the folds of his brightly coloured Arab robes. 'Please, not to keep him waiting.' The dark eyebrows were pulled together in a knowing look.

From where she was standing she could see a number of tables, where the evening visitors were relaxing over drinks. She recognised no one. Her spirits rose.

'You'll have to take me over and point out the doctor,' she told the driver.

The driver ushered her across the room and stopped beside a table where an Egyptian in a dark grey suit was sipping a glass of fruit juice.

'This is the doctor.'

Penny's spirits rose even higher.

The Egyptian leapt to his feet and held out his hand. 'You must be Sister Byrne. We've been expecting you.'

'And you must be Dr Hamilton,' Penny replied happily, shaking the stranger's outstretched hand.

The doctor smiled as he shook his head. 'Forgive me. I am Dr Ahmed Fakry. I'm in charge of the clinic here. Dr Hamilton is our boss, the co-ordinator of our medical organisation. But we are fortunate that he is staying with us for a few weeks. Ah, here he is. . .'

Her legs were turning to jelly; her empty stomach churned on its vacuum; she tried to speak but her voice came out in an unfamiliar squeak.

'How do you do, Dr Hamilton?' She avoided eye contact with the tall man who had just joined them.

Dr Hamilton, unlike his subordinate, didn't hold out a welcoming hand. He merely sank into a chair at the other side of the table from Penny and gave her a curt nod.

'Good evening, Sister. We expected you an hour ago.'

Oh, she would remember that voice anywhere! How many times had she wakened in the night and remembered those honeyed, seductive tones? But now there was a cool professionalism in the sound.

'The plane was late; the taxi was long past its sell-by date,' she answered firmly, wondering why on earth she should be apologising to this pompous man after her long day. It wasn't her fault if the travel arrangements had been inefficient.

Clive Hamilton was studying a file of papers. She could only see the top of his head. That black hair she'd found so attractive as a young student nurse hadn't changed colour. But as he raised his head she saw the most infinitesimal touch of grey around his temple, reminding her that he must now be approaching forty. Yes, he'd told her he was thirty-four on that first encounter. And she'd been an innocent twenty-year-old, young, unsophisticated, untried. . .until he came along. . .

He seemed to look through her now.

'According to your file you were appointed as our second choice. The first candidate dropped out at the last moment.'

She nodded. 'That's correct. I'm between jobs with three months to spare before I take up my next assignment. My name is on the register at the nursing agency for short-term work. When they phoned to see if I could do a last-minute assignment in Egypt I naturally jumped at the chance.'

She realised that she was talking too quickly, running out of breath. At any moment the great doctor would surely take a further look at her and then the explanations would have to begin...on both sides. But she wasn't going to be the first one to open up the can of worms.

'Why?' he barked.

My God! He was still handsome, even when he looked fierce.

'Why what?' she countered, still avoiding those sexy grey eyes that had been her downfall.

'Why did you jump at the chance?'

'Well—er—I've always wanted to go to Egypt, ever since I saw *Antony and Cleopatra* on the TV. It seems such an exciting place, full of mystery and...' Her voice petered out as she saw the patronising glances of the two men.

'There's a lot of work to be done here,' Clive Hamilton said suavely. 'We don't need a romantic view of Egypt. We need someone with their feet planted firmly on the ground. Someone who won't get carried away by emotion and...'

Now it was the doctor's words that faltered. For a split second their eyes met and she knew he remembered her. How could he forget?

'But it helps if you feel an affinity with a country,' she retorted, aware that she was blustering. She leaned back against the seat and gave an involuntary sigh.

'You must be tired, Sister, after your long journey,' Dr Fakry interposed. 'Let me offer you some refreshment. A glass of *karkaday*, perhaps? It is one of the drinks with which we welcome visitors to our country.'

She smiled. 'Thank you.' It was good to know that one of the doctors had some good manners!

A waiter in dazzling white brought a tall glass filled with the purple-coloured juice over from the bar. It had a delicate taste of hibiscus which Penny found most refreshing. She was aware that Clive Hamilton was watching her surreptitiously while she drank.

Sizing me up! she thought, keeping her eyes deliberately downcast. Checking out if I've changed in five years. Oh, yes, I've changed. . .thanks to you! The sweet little creature you knew no longer exists.

'When you've finished your drink, perhaps you'd like to see the clinic. It's built into the hotel on the ground floor so that it becomes immediately available to the tourists,' Clive Hamilton said in a nonchalant voice.

'I'd rather have a shower and settle into my room. Tomorrow morning I shall feel fit enough to start work here,' Penny said, standing up. 'Thank you for the drink, Dr Fakry. Good night, gentlemen.'

The men rose to their feet as she left them. She was aware of the stunned expression on Clive Hamilton's face. He was not a man who was used to having his ideas dismissed out of hand.

Do him good! she thought as she strode over to the reception desk to collect her key. It's time someone put him in his place. Nevertheless, she felt relieved when the lift doors closed. She half expected Dr Hamilton to call her back.

The porter carried her luggage and opened the door of her room on the fourth floor. She was drawn at once to the wide window. Opening the floor-length casement, she went out on to the balcony and looked out across the Nile to the west bank. Night had fallen, but the myriad lights from the huge cruise ships and tiny white-sailed feluccas on the Nile created a continually fascinating rainbow kaleidoscope. And high above the ghostly waving palm trees a new moon was trying hard to emulate the sun.

'Oh, it's so beautiful!' she breathed, to no one in particular.

From the interior of her room, she heard a slight cough and remembered the porter. She went back inside. The porter appeared more than happy with the notes she handed over.

Got to get this money sorted out, she thought as the door closed behind the young man. She enjoyed being generous, but it wouldn't do to run out of money in this foreign land. And she had no reserves, no nest-egg from previous savings.

Money had always been scarce in her family. With two younger brothers and two younger sisters, she'd got used to being careful. Her mother had seen to that! There had never been anything left over for luxuries. But there had been plenty of love and laughter.

Through all the skimping and scraping of her

childhood, she never remembered her mother's spirits flagging.

'Oh, something will turn up,' her mother had declared when there wasn't enough food in the house and the Friday wage packet was two days away.

And it always had.

The knock on the door broke through her fond reminiscences. Penny froze.

'Who is it?'

'Clive Hamilton.'

She drew in her breath. It was impossible to conduct a conversation through the door even if she wanted to. He was her boss, after all. She would have to let him in.

As she opened the door he strode in. One glance told her that he was angry. He marched over to the window and sank down into one of the armchairs, motioning her to join him.

She frowned. This was her room. He couldn't just walk in and take over even if he was her boss.

'Now wait a minute. . .' she began, remaining by the open door. 'I wasn't aware that I'd invited you up here, Dr Hamilton.'

'Close the door and come over here. . .please, Penny.'

His voice had mellowed. He was looking directly at her and she felt again the pull of attraction she'd once known. Reluctantly she complied, moving towards him ever so slowly so as to think how she was going to handle the situation. The way he'd said, 'Please, Penny' left her in no doubt that he had total recall of their last encounter.

'So you remember me,' she said, quietly sitting down.

She was only inches away from him now. They were totally alone. She could see the granite structure of his tanned face glowing with sensual vitality. She remembered he was a health fanatic, jogging in the mornings, working out at the gymnasium, constantly trying to push back his age. . .and succeeding, because she had to admit that he was in perfect physical condition. If anything, he was even more handsome than the last time she'd seen him. He had the look of a man who had lived a lot, possibly suffered, but emerged triumphant, a man who knew what he wanted from life. . .and made damn sure he got it!

'Oh, yes, I remember you,' he said huskily. 'I'm curious to know why you came out here. All that baloney about *Antony and Cleopatra* didn't fool me. Did you know I was in charge out here?'

She bridled. 'You flatter yourself if you think I followed you out here. It was an unpleasant shock when I read your name on the prospectus.'

She saw the muscle of his jaw quiver and wished she hadn't been quite so harsh. But then he deserved it. It was merely a verbal slap in the face and he'd had it coming to him for a long time.

He drew in his breath. 'Well, at least we know where we stand.'

The phone was ringing. He moved across the

room. 'I'll get that. I told the clinic I'd be up here for a few minutes.'

His face took on a serious expression. 'Yes, I'll come at once.' He put down the phone and faced her, his brow furrowed, his eyes narrowing.

'That was the clinic. An emergency admission. It's a pity you're too tired because we could do with an extra pair of hands.'

He was opening the door. She hesitated, but only for a brief moment.

'I think I could force myself to work if you really need me.'

His mouth quivered as he smiled down at her. His eyes, she noticed, held a sensuously tender expression. . .an expression that she'd remembered in her mind on so many occasions as she'd tantalised herself with the thought of what might have been if only he hadn't disappeared from her life.

'That's my girl,' he said quietly.

She shook her head. 'No, you're wrong. This is a purely professional decision, Dr Hamilton.'

His smile grew even broader. 'You haven't changed, Penny.'

'Neither have you.'

He reached out his hand towards her. 'It's a pity we have work to do.'

A slow blush spread across her face as she ignored his hand and brushed past him. 'Let's go!'

CHAPTER TWO

THE outside of the clinic was made almost entirely of glass set into the ground floor of the hotel. Penny hurried in through the outer door and found herself in a low-ceilinged, white-painted reception area. The young Egyptian nurse at the reception desk leapt to her feet. Ignoring Penny, she approached Clive.

'Dr Hamilton, thank goodness you're here. Staff Nurse Rania, our trained nurse on duty, had to go home because her mother is sick; Dr Fakry is off duty and——'

'That's OK, Samira, our new sister has arrived.'

As he introduced her, Penny could feel the nurse sizing her up. She wondered if there was any resentment about the fact that she, a foreigner, would waltz in and take charge for three months.

'Welcome, Sister Byrne,' the girl said in a solemn voice. 'If you would like to come this way I will show you where you can change into your uniform.'

'There's no time for that, Samira,' Clive Hamilton broke in impatiently. 'I thought we were going to deal with an emergency. Where's the patient?'

'In here, sir.' Samira moved quickly towards the door, hurrying through into a small treatment-room where a motionless figure lay on the examination couch, covered by a sheet. The blonde-haired woman's eyes were open, but they held a frightened expression. She turned to look at the doctor and his nursing sister.

'I'm so sorry, Doctor. It's all my fault. I know I should have stayed at home...then none of this would have happened. I'm going to lose the baby, aren't I?'

Penny had reached the examination couch and she put her hand down on the patient's forehead. 'Now hush, my dear. You're in good hands. Just tell us what's happened to you.'

Clive Hamilton, standing across the other side of the examination couch, reached across and put his finger on the woman's wrist, feeling for her pulse. In his other hand he held the thin sheet of notes that the reception nurse had handed him.

'Well, Sarah, I see you're staying here in the hotel. Your husband James, is he here with you?'

The patient shook her head. 'He's gone to Aswan for a couple of days on business.' She grimaced and put her hand over her stomach.

'Let's take a look, shall we?' Clive said, leaning over the patient.

Penny had located some sterile gloves and she helped Clive to put on a pair. Their fingers inevitably brushed and she felt the strange tugging at her heartstrings, this impossible-to-understand feeling of simultaneous love and hate. But there was no time to worry about their relationship. The patient was all that mattered at the moment and this poor woman was going to require their joint skills.

Clive's examination revealed that Sarah Greenwood was six months pregnant but suffering from intense uterine contractions. It seemed as if a premature labour couldn't be avoided.

Penny drew in her breath, trying not to show her anxiety. At twenty-six weeks the foetus might be viable, but the chances were very slim indeed. She'd once delivered a baby at twenty-eight weeks which had survived, but that was in a London teaching hospital with all the latest technological equipment. What kind of chance would this wee mite have out here? Her eyes met Clive's and she saw the same misgivings etched on his face. And even in this dire emergency she couldn't help noticing the look of compassion on his face, that expression that she'd first seen when he'd bent over a terminal patient during his lecture tour all those years ago. It was good to remind herself that the man was human after all and not some demon from the past come to haunt her.

He was motioning her to move away from the examination couch. Outside the cubicle he briefed her in a tense, urgent voice.

'I'm going to try a new drug to prevent a premature labour. Can I count on your support?'

Her eyebrows shot up. 'Is this a dangerous drug?'

He frowned. 'Not half so dangerous as allowing the foetus to be expelled fourteen weeks before term. Inside that uterus is an immature foetus, ill equipped to breathe. In an ideal hospital situation we might just be able to save it, but it stands no chance out here. I know the facilities of the various hospitals and——'

'How about Cairo?' Penny's question held a note of desperation.

Clive shook his head. 'We'd never get her there in time.' He took a deep breath, as if indicating that his mind was made up. 'I've got to stop the premature labour now. This new drug has recently been given a clean bill of health so I'm going to use it. Bring over an IV stand and a sterile IV packet while I explain to our patient what's going to happen.'

'So you're not going to give her any alternative? You're just going to go ahead and say this is the correct treatment?'

He put his hands forward and placed them on either side of her shoulders. Even in this anxious situation she felt a *frisson* of excitement running down her spine at the touch of his fingers.

'Do you, as a woman, think I should give her the option of choosing?'

'But of course!'

His mouth turned up at the corners and his eyes lost their look of desperation.

'Why is it that women can see things so much more clearly than men? Situations are either right or wrong. . .black or white. OK, you win. . .but bring over the equipment so that I can set up the IV as soon as I've persuaded our patient. I'm going to wheel her into one of the side-wards through that door over there.'

Penny gave him a whimsical smile. He was going to give the patient the option of choosing, but at the same time persuade her into his way of thinking. And with a strong character like Clive Hamilton it was difficult to say no. What he wanted he made sure he got, in his professional as well as his private life.

It took her a couple of minutes to gather up all the equipment necessary to set up the IV. When she returned with her fully laden trolley she found the patient was practically eating out of Clive's hand. In spite of the pain caused by the premature contractions, Sarah Greenwood was smiling bravely up into the eyes of the handsome doctor and acquiescing to everything he was recommending.

'Oh, yes, I agree, Doctor. . . Well, I'll put myself entirely into your hands. . . You know best.'

Only Penny saw the faint look of apprehension that crossed Clive's face. Only she knew that, however confident he might seem on the exterior, inside there remained a certain doubt, the inevitable 'what if. . .' that haunted doctors who were trying out a new technique.

'Well, in view of your age, Sarah. . .' Clive was saying, and Penny glanced down at the notes to find that their patient was forty-one and this was her first baby after three miscarriages. So Clive was wise to try to bring this one to full term or at least as near as they could get. Otherwise the poor little foetus might finish up as a statistical fourth miscarriage. And Sarah Greenwood, having turned the big four O, might decide she'd had enough of trying for a baby.

Penny swabbed the patient's arm in preparation for the insertion of the cannula. She took the wrapping from the bottle containing the new intravenous drug which would stop the contractions. It was a patented name that she'd read about only recently in the *Nursing Times*. She remembered now hearing that it had been given the all-clear after much controversy. She only hoped Clive knew what he was doing...but then why should she doubt him? He might be a swine in his love-life, but no one had ever questioned his professional expertise and integrity. At least, not when she was around.

'We'll have to keep you here for a few days, Sarah,' Clive said, straightening his back at the end of the treatment. 'Sister Byrne and I will stay with you throughout this first night so don't worry. As soon as the contractions start to disappear I'll give you a mild sedative and you can go to sleep.'

A couple of hours later, as they sat in the doctors' office drinking coffee, Penny reflected that their patient had no idea what a nail-biting time it had been until the contractions started to subside. She had monitored the foetal heartbeat continually for signs of distress. This would have been a direct indication to discontinue the treatment and let nature take its course, which would have been to expel this frail and probably unviable foetus. But, in the event, the foetal heartbeat had remained strong. The contractions had disappeared completely and, after a mild sedative, their patient had drifted happily off to sleep, secure in the knowledge that this was one baby that might reach full term.

'A very interesting case,' Clive said, putting his cup down on the desk and looking across at Penny, who was curled in an armchair underneath the ceiling fan.

There was air-conditioning throughout the clinic, but the addition of a ceiling fan in strategically placed areas made the temperature all the more comfortable, and the slight breeze was always welcome, making breathing seem easier in the dry heat.

Penny took a sip of her coffee. 'Sarah opened up and practically told me her life history just before I gave her the sedative. Apparently, it's her second marriage. She had three miscarriages before her first marriage broke up. Her first husband took off with his secretary. When she'd recovered from the shock she divorced him and then fell in love soon afterwards with James. His job entails a lot of travelling and she insists on going with him. She freely admits that she's scared to let him out of her sight in case he too decides to find a younger woman. He's only thirty-one, ten years younger than her, and she's fed up with the predictable jokes about taking a toy boy. As you can imagine, this is a much wanted baby. I dearly hope we can save it. And I hope we haven't raised her hopes higher than they should be.'

Clive's eyes flickered, but his gaze remained steady. 'Optimism in a patient is no bad thing. And if the worst happens. . .well, we'll just have to deal with that eventuality. And it's much better to have a patient who's feeling positive than one who's worried. Nobody should have to worry unnecessarily. Cross each bridge when you come to it and don't look too far ahead.'

'Is that your general philosophy in life?'

He gave her a long, slow, tantalising smile. 'It depends on the situation. Who would have thought that it would have taken all these years for our paths to cross again?'

She bridled. 'Yes, who would have thought it?' she answered in a cool, unemotional voice.

'I suppose leaving it to chance, as we did, we couldn't expect to meet again,' he drawled, standing up and moving over towards her.

Leaving it to chance, my eye! she thought as she watched him approaching. It was all clear-cut before he'd gone away. He was going to write. . . He was going to phone. . . He was going to. . .

His hands were reaching out towards her and this was for real. This wasn't a dream from which she would awake bathed in sweat and wishing she'd never clapped eyes on the elusive Clive Hamilton. She uncurled her legs in one swift motion, but he was too quick for her. Reaching down, he scooped her into his arms, pressing his lips against hers. For a brief moment she struggled and then her lips parted in acquiescence.

She revelled in the feeling of the hot, damp skin of his face pressed against hers. She remembered that his body was covered in thick, dark hair; a mental image of his broad, muscular chest flashed into her mind and now as the dark stubble of his chin chafed her she found the discomfort exquisite. She closed her eyes to savour the moment. . .and that was all it was. . .a moment.

A moment in which time had stood still and she'd lost her head again. He was staring down at her with a tenderly appealing expression on his charismatic face.

'It's been a long time, Penny. What's been happening to you over in London?'

She eased herself out of his arms and sank back into the armchair, making it quite clear that she didn't want him to renew contact. When she spoke she had to make a determined effort to control her voice.

'I finished my training and stayed on at St Celine's first as a staff nurse and then as a sister.'

He was moving away, going back to his desk. Penny's sigh of relief was tinged with sadness. She watched the broad back, the dark hair falling almost to the collar-line of his white coat. He looked so young. . .and then he swung around, his face revealing the lines of maturity that showed he'd lived at a fast pace.

'And boyfriends? I expected you'd be married by now, probably having your own kids. You didn't strike me as being the career type.'

'Oh, you know, love 'em and leave 'em, that's me,' she replied glibly. If he was going to be superficial, so was she! She wasn't going to reveal how much their brief affair had affected her, how every other man she'd been out with just hadn't matched up.

'So, having risen to the rank of sister at St Celine's—and the competition is fierce, I know that—how come you've got a spare three months before moving on to another assignment?'

She hesitated. 'I wanted to travel. . .to see the

world. I felt it was time to move on from the hospital where I'd trained. So I resigned and put my name on the register at the London Agency. They told me that ICMWT had an immediate vacancy for three months—and you know the rest.'

'But why did you become suddenly disenchanted with London? I don't understand it. You seemed to have everything going for you and——'

'Please, Clive, leave it at that. This is turning into an inquisition.'

'I'm sorry; I didn't mean to upset you.'

She found his mellifluous voice even more disturbing than his harsh interrogation.

'Isn't it time we went back to check on Sarah?'

'She'll sleep for hours now that the contractions have disappeared. A two-hourly check on bloodpressure and foetal heartbeat is all that's necessary. You can go to bed if you like. I can cope down here. Nurse Samira will help me if necessary. She's only an auxiliary nurse, but she's very intelligent and willing to learn.'

'Yes, I was wondering about the staff situation here. I would have expected there to be a trained nurse at all times.'

He smiled. 'Theoretically there is. It's you, the sister in charge. You're on twenty-four-hour call. . . no, hear me out, Penny.'

Penny's raised eyebrows had registered her protest, but she remained silent as he gave her an explanation.

'As I said, the sister in charge is on twenty-four-hour call, but that doesn't mean she has to be here all the time. There are two trained staff nurses, Rania and Nadia, who come in either from eight in the morning till four or from four in the afternoon till midnight. They take alternate weekly shifts. You're here to supervise their work as and when you feel it necessary. But you've got to be on call between midnight and four. I may add that our permanent sister was unwilling to give up the post, but she's expecting her first baby and we gave her three months' maternity leave. She'll be back before Christmas, so don't worry, you won't miss your English Christmas dinner.'

Penny's eyes flickered. That was the least of her worries! 'And what hours does Nurse Samira work?'

'She's our night receptionist this week. She alternates with Fatima, this week's day receptionist. Dr Fakry is on permanent call, but I told him to take advantage of the fact that I'm here for a few weeks and take some off duty. If we get exceptionally busy the local hospital can usually provide extra staff. It's rarely necessary, but we do liaise closely with them. We can perform minor emergency operations here in our small operating theatre, but any major surgery is performed at the hospital here or in Cairo or in the UK if there's time to get the patient on a plane.'

She stood up. 'Well, if I'm on permanent call, I'd better get some sleep. I must admit I'm dead on my feet. It's been a long, long day since Gatwick airport.'

He pulled himself to his feet and moved quickly around the desk, stopping in front of her so that she couldn't reach for the door-handle. Her heart was thumping madly. She avoided his eyes as she tried to push past him.

He was leaning against the door, his eyes glinting dangerously.

'At least it's a relief to find you still like me,' he said softly.

'Whatever gave you that idea?' she flung at him. 'If you're referring to the way you kissed me just now, then——'

'Oh, come on, Penny. I can tell when a girl fancies me. I felt your response just now and. . .'

His voice stopped as Penny administered a well aimed slap to his face. 'You're a conceited brute. . . and I wish I'd never met you. If I'd had the slightest hint that you might be out here I would have stayed in England.'

She was appalled at the tears that suddenly started to flow down her cheeks. She was dead tired and her emotions were running out of control.

He reached for her and pulled her roughly against his chest. His hands stroked her back soothingly, as if she were a child. She didn't resist. How could she? She was emotionally exhausted and the comfort of this safe haven was all she needed for the moment. It didn't make sense to capitulate like this, but she would worry about that later.

And now he was kissing her again. The salt of her tears mingled with the exquisite taste of his lips. His tongue probed gently and then more fiercely. She felt the sensual response that quivered through her. Now was the time to break off if she wasn't to reach the point of no return. . .as she had done before with this tantalising monster.

'No, Clive. . .no!' She struggled in his arms and he let her go, a confident smile on his lips.

'Why the sudden virginal stance? Are you planning to go into a nunnery after you finish here?'

She smiled back, summoning up all her inner strength for a few brief moments.

'Just because you seduced me on our last date, it doesn't mean you'll succeed second time around.'

He gave a hoarse laugh. 'Seduced you? Come on, Penny. You wanted it as much as I did. We made love, remember? At least, that's what I thought.'

'I don't remember what happened,' she lied, as the mental images flashed through her mind. Her body almost betrayed her as she remembered the exquisite feeling of Clive's skin against her own, his muscles rippling against hers, his strong, thrusting thighs as he drove her on to an ecstatic climax.

'Don't you remember crying out that you loved me?' he whispered hoarsely.

She lifted her moist eyes to his and her expression betrayed her.

'Of course you remember,' he said, a sardonic smile playing on his lips. 'But you're tired now. Go to bed.' He flung open the door and stood aside. 'Get some sleep. Goodnight, Penny.'

She pushed past him, willing herself to remain calm.

Alone in her room, she tried hard to sleep, but although she was desperately tired her mind wouldn't switch off.

She remembered so clearly their brief affair. Clive had come to St Celine's as a visiting lecturer on tropical medicine. And the minute he'd mounted the rostrum in the lecture theatre he'd captivated everyone. It seemed as if all her colleagues had fallen for him — even the married ones!

She sat up in bed and put on the bedside lamp. Three o'clock. . .oh, ye gods, would she ever sleep? She looked around the unfamiliar room. It was certainly a step up from her bed-sit in Battersea. Rich, dark, aubergine-coloured silk curtains draped the windows; a couple of luxuriously comfortable armchairs were placed beside a cedar-wood coffee-table. It was a double room. She looked across at the other bed and envisaged what it would be like to be married to someone like Clive. She smiled. Someone like Clive wouldn't want to sleep in twin beds! Clive would insist on a huge king-size bed and they would make love all night. . .as they had done on their last night together.

She drew in her breath as the memories flooded back. Why Clive had ever asked her out when he could have had the pick of the hospital she had no idea. But he'd singled her out on that first morning when they'd broken for coffee. He'd walked across the room, threading his way through the crowd of medics and nurses until he was standing in front of her. And their eyes had met. . .

She sighed as she snuggled back against the pillows. What was it he'd said? 'I noticed you seem particularly interested in tropical medicine. At least, every time I looked your way you were giving me your undivided attention. Are you planning to travel when you've completed your training, Nurse?'

And she'd replied, 'I'm not sure, sir.' And the room had seemed to go oh, so still, as if all eyes were upon her, and most of them envying her for being the centre of Clive Hamilton's attention.

After lunch he'd left the senior-medical-staff table and approached her again. Would she like to have dinner with him that evening? Would she indeed! But she'd managed to remain cool on the outside as she'd accepted his invitation.

She stretched out now and lay still, looking up at the high white ceiling. She'd believed it had been love at first sight. Clive's grey eyes had held such magic as he looked at her across the table of the riverside restaurant. The lights twinkling on the Thames barges had been lit just for them. . .to add to the illusion that they were in a fairy-tale wonderland. All around them people moved, ate, talked, but the world had ceased to exist as they got to know each other.

And afterwards he'd taken her back to his hotel room and she'd willingly lost her virginity in his kingsize bed. It seemed so predictable on reflection — an older man seducing a young girl — but it hadn't been like that. She'd been young, inexperienced, but something inside her had told her that this was the man of her dreams, the man who would be with her for the rest of her life. . .her ideal man. . .

How wrong could she have been? His promises that he would contact her were empty. And from being the envy of the hospital, she became the object of pity and amusement. She thought she'd fallen in love, but she'd only fallen for the oldest trick in the book. But she'd paid the price by becoming cynical and over-cautious where men were concerned. Her naturally outgoing nature had undergone a profound change. She now suspected all men of having an ulterior motive.

Turning to switch off the light, she closed her eyes and lay back against the cool sheet. As far as boyfriends were concerned, she'd never met anyone she'd wanted to fall in love with. The affair with Clive had shown her what romance was really about . . .even if it had all been false.

Across the Nile she heard the eerie sound of the speakers from one of the tall, thin minaret towers. She'd read in her guidebook that five times a day the mosque officials known as muezzins bellowed out the call to prayer through these speakers. Faithful Muslims followed this call and filled the mosques below for several minutes of elaborate prayers. It must be almost dawn.

As she drifted off into an uneasy slumber she vowed that she wouldn't fall for Clive's false charms again. Second time around she was going to be much wiser.

CHAPTER THREE

THE sun was warm as Penny stepped out on to her balcony. She'd managed to sleep for a few hours and she felt refreshed and ready to face whatever the day threw at her. . .including Clive Hamilton. The boats were moving up and down the Nile, causing wide ripples of water to merge in fascinating channels. The tiny feluccas pushed their way between the huge pleasure boats, ducking and diving like birds on a busy pond.

Penny could see that the breeze that fanned their sails was welcome in a September day that promised to turn into another Egyptian scorcher.

She turned as she heard the tapping on the door. Crossing back inside the luxurious room, she padded to the door.

'Your breakfast, *madame*.'

The white-coated waiter carried a tray high on his shoulders into the room, setting it down on the low coffee-table.

'But I didn't order breakfast,' she began, looking at the vast array of food: a varied selection of cheeses, boiled eggs, toast, croissants, an assortment of preserves. . .and two cups beside the large coffee-pot.

'The doctor said. . .' The waiter's voice petered away as his eyes focused on a spot behind her head.

She turned, wrapping her housecoat closer to her as she saw her unannounced morning visitor.

'I hope we didn't waken you,' Clive said, walking with confident strides across the room and settling himself into one of the armchairs. 'I thought a professional discussion over breakfast would save time. I've got to go over to Hurghada on the Red Sea today and I won't be able to see you later. Do come and join me. . .and don't look so annoyed. As I said, this is purely a professional visit.'

'Hadn't it occurred to you that I might prefer to breakfast alone?'

Clive smiled as he handed over some *baksheesh* to the waiter, who retreated quickly and closed the door behind him.

'Indeed it had, but you'll have to get used to the fact that you've left the comforts of home in England. This is Egypt and we rise with the dawn so as to get on with our work before the heat becomes too oppressive.'

She swallowed her annoyance and sank down into one of the two armchairs, wrapping her white cotton broderie anglaise robe around her. But she noticed that even though Clive was busy with the coffee-pot he managed to cast a glance across in her direction, and the expression in his eyes melted away some of her icy defence mechanism.

She took the cup of coffee he was handing to her. As her fingers brushed his she felt a shiver of sensual arousal. But she stifled the feeling. Clive was yesterday's love and she was interested only in today and tomorrow. He was a part of her past that she preferred to forget.

'Try the croissants. They're the best I've tasted outside Paris,' Clive said, handing over the large plate. 'As I was saying, I've got to go to Hurghada. Pity you can't come with me, but someone has to hold the fort. Ahmed Fakry will be here to help you and the staff nurses are very reliable. Our emergency patient is improving, but I'd like to have a word with her husband when he gets back from his business trip, so see if you can set that up for me, will you? The morning surgery should be fairly routine, but then you never can tell in this climate. If you have any problems that you can't handle, the hospital. . .'

Penny was fascinated by his deep, husky and innately sexy voice and was having difficulty in concentrating. It had been the same on that first morning when he'd stood on the rostrum of the lecture theatre. His voice was so melodious, so full of differing cadences, that it could enthral and captivate her without her having taken in the meaning of the words. But she made a valiant effort to keep her attention on the important points in his instructions, even breaking off to find a pen and make notes.

She could see that he was pleased by this show of dedication. . .or was he merely watching the way her robe swung open when she sat down? She pulled it closer around her neckline with her left hand while trying to write with her right. This seemed to amuse him, because his eyes were dancing with a tantalising expression when she looked up.

'I really think you're planning to quit nursing and join a religious order,' he said. 'Anyone would think I'd never seen a woman's body before. Stop being such a puritan, Penny. It doesn't suit you.'

She faced him with a stony expression. 'You mean it's like locking the stable door after the horse has bolted?'

His eyes clouded over with a worried expression. 'I didn't say that.' He reached across the table, but she moved, adroitly avoiding his searching fingers.

The phone was ringing. She picked it up, glad of the interruption.

'Hello, Victor! Why are you phoning? Has something happened?'

The laughter in the voice of her friend in England came floating over the wires. 'Do we have to have a catastrophe before I can phone my girlfriend?'

'But it's so expensive.'

Again the laugh. 'I'm not paying. Dad won't be in the surgery for ages yet and the practice phone bill is always astronomical. Nobody's going to worry about one little international call. How's it going out there?'

'Fine.' She was intensely aware of Clive's eyes upon her, and he was trying to attract her attention.

'I've got to go,' he whispered. 'Give my regards to Victor...'

The door was opening, then closing.

'Who's there with you?' the voice on the phone asked. 'It sounds like a man.'

'He's gone... It was just one of the waiters clearing away my breakfast.'

'Oh... Why did he send his regards to me?'

She gave a sigh of exasperation. 'Oh, well, if you must know, there's been the most amazing coincidence. The co-ordinator of the medical group out here is Clive Hamilton.'

There was silence at the other end of the phone.

'Victor, are you still there?'

'No, I've thrown myself through the window.'

'Look, I had no idea...but anyway it's got nothing to do with you any more. You and I are just good friends...always have been...'

'Thanks to Dr Clive Superman Hamilton.'

'Now, Victor, that's not true and you know it. There never was anything between us. Clive Hamilton turned up five years ago and we had a brief affair. I don't know why...it just happened and——'

'And who was left to pick up the pieces?' came the brisk reply.

'Victor, you were wonderful at the time. I admit I couldn't have got through without you. But that's all over now. I'm a completely different character now. I won't make the same mistake twice.'

'Won't you?'

Penny bridled at the sarcastic inflexion in Victor's voice. He knew her so well! Dear Victor; what would she have done without him five years ago when she had been bleeding from the results of her brief affair with Clive...yes, literally bleeding.

'I'll try not to,' she breathed into the phone.

'He's a swine.' Victor's voice echoed her sentiments exactly.

'I know!'

'Then, having discovered the situation out there, don't you think you'd better come back to London? They still haven't filled your post. I had to go up to London to visit one of our patients in St Celine's and I listened in on the gossip. Apparently that temporary sister isn't competent enough. They're going to have to get someone more permanent. Someone with experience. . .like you.'

'Hang on a minute. You're the one who pushed me out here in the first place. You're the one who said I should travel, get out of London and stop brooding. Who sent me the ad in the *Nursing Times* and told me to apply. . .to broaden my horizons? I thought you were trying to get rid of me.'

The familiar laugh came down the phone. 'OK, I admit it. But I didn't know old Bluebeard would be there. So now that you've discovered your honour might be compromised a second time, how do you feel?'

She took a deep breath. 'I'm going to stay, Victor. It's only for three months. Then I'll come back and take up my post again. You told me I was getting in a rut, that I needed to get away. . .see the world.'

She heard the groan at the other end of the phone and could just imagine Victor's brown eyes rolling up towards the ceiling. He was one of the most patient men she'd ever met, but even he could get exasperated at times. But never with the patients. He was always the kindest, most considerate doctor. It had been the same when he was a medical student.

They were the same age, from the same home

town, Liverpool. They'd often met on the bus going home from school and found out they were doing the same A levels. Then they had both gone off to London to the same teaching hospital and the friendship had continued.

Victor's father was the Byrne family's GP and it had been a foregone conclusion that Victor would join the family practice. It hadn't occurred to Penny to become a doctor. Her examination grades were as good as Victor's, but she was a girl, and her family made sure she knew her place. Doctors, according to the Byrne family, were traditionally men, and girls would be overstepping themselves if they tried to compete.

She wasn't complaining. By the time she'd realised she could have got a place at medical school she had already been enjoying her life as a student nurse. And with Victor as a medical student she had always been invited to the medical balls and the social activities at the university union. But, little by little, she had outgrown him. He no longer interested her. . . She found him boring. And she was glad that she'd actively discouraged any physical contact. He'd always been a surrogate brother to her.

But he'd been marvellous when Clive ditched her. She'd told him everything and he'd lent a sympathetic ear. He hadn't criticised her. There was no question of him saying that he'd told her so, that she'd been out of her depth. . .

In the middle of her reminiscences she realised that Victor hadn't reacted to her announcement that she was going to stay.

'Are you still there, Victor?'

'Yes. . . I was just wondering what I could do to persuade you to pack up and come home. I really miss you, Penny.'

She wished she could say the same. But in all honesty she couldn't. Even with the materialisation of Clive Hamilton—perhaps because of this new situation—she had no intention of going back to the UK.

'Three months will pass very quickly,' she replied in a brisk tone. 'Aren't you enjoying work in the family practice?'

'Oh, it's good to be back among our old friends. That's about all you can say. The older patients tend to treat me as if I'm still at school. . .the ones who've known me since I was a child, that is. The newcomers still don't know what to make of me. I'm thinking of growing a beard and painting a few wrinkles on my face.

For a moment, she was struck with a pang of nostalgia . . . The old crowd from school days. . .all married by now and pushing prams. . .and her mother's cosy kitchen. . .the raw wind blowing across the river on a Sunday afternoon's walk. . .

'I don't want to go back to live. . .not yet awhile,' she said in a convincing tone. 'But I'm glad you did. Your father always wanted you to work with him.'

'Let's see how you feel in three months, Penny.'

The phone went dead. She put it back on its cradle and strode over to the window. This spectacular view of the Nile was beginning to feel like home to her. It was nothing like the muddy old Mersey, but still it was a river...and she'd grown up beside a river. She'd been hoisted shoulder-high so that she could watch the ocean-going vessels sailing off to foreign parts. And now here she was, little Penny, all by herself in as foreign a part as you could wish for.

She had to see the thing through...because only then could she lay the ghost to rest. The enigma of Clive Hamilton had been haunting her ever since he'd taken off and left her stranded.

She moved out on to the balcony and stood with her hands on the balustrade. Her knuckles tightened as she told herself that Clive hadn't known she was pregnant when he'd taken off. Neither had she.

She swallowed hard as she remembered her unaccountable elation when she'd missed her first period...then her second. That this should happen to her was incredible. She'd kept herself all through those teenage days for the man she knew she would marry. So many of her girlfriends had recounted to her stories of wonderful sensuous experiences, implying that she didn't know what she was missing by holding out.

But she'd smiled and told her friends that she had old-fashioned values instilled in her by her Catholic mother. She herself had never been religious, but some of the philosophy and morals of the nuns at the convent had rubbed off on her. And she'd always planned to remain a virgin until her wedding night.

And then along came Clive Hamilton and changed all her ideas in one evening. Over the last five years she'd justified her actions by remembering that she'd been convinced this was the man for her. He was the only man who'd ever made her feel like that. And for that evening she'd given no thought about what might come afterwards. In her own mind she'd been sure they would marry and live happily ever after. . .

She sighed now, as she looked down on the broad expanse of swimming-pool that bordered the Nile. The hotel guests were drifting out after breakfast, spreading themselves on the wide, comfortable sun-loungers, raising their languorous arms to attract the attention of a waiter and order some coffee. . .

She turned away from the leisured scene and went back into her room. The maid had arrived and was stripping off the sheets from her bed, replacing them with crisp white cotton straight from the laundry. What an extravagance! She'd only slept in them once. At home, her mother would have put them top to bottom at the end of the week if she were lucky. . .

She went into the bathroom, assuring the maid that it was OK to carry on. She was going to take a quick shower before going on duty.

As she turned on the water she told herself that she'd been a fool to believe Clive Hamilton's honeyed words as he'd made love to her. She had to turn up the water now to convince herself and blot out the exquisite memories of that virile body entwined with hers.

She soaped her skin vigorously as she remembered how he'd told her he would write. He couldn't give her an address because he was going out into the middle of the West African bush. But as soon as he was settled he would let her know where he was. And he would phone. If there was the remotest chance of him having a phone number on his travels he would let her have it.

'Huh!' The exclamation brought her nothing except a mouthful of soapy water and the familiar feeling of having been let down as she remembered how she'd continued to hope, to believe that Clive was all that he'd seemed to be on that heavenly night.

And then the bombshell! The realisation that she was pregnant. And against all sensible ideas she'd found that she was thrilled, excited, longing only to hear from Clive so that she could tell him. When she'd missed her second period she'd confided in Victor.

He'd been oh, so kind. Without him. . .

A lone tear escaped and ran down her cheek with the shampoo from her hair. Victor had been patience itself, telling her to forget Clive, even saying that he wanted to marry her. . .that he would accept it as his own baby.

She put her hand on her wet stomach, now flat and firm, but then just beginning to swell with Clive's baby. She'd assured Victor that this was a much wanted baby, that it was only a question of time before Clive contacted her. He was unaccountably delayed in the African bush. . . Africa was a big continent. . .

She stepped out of the shower and dried herself vigorously, trying to erase the memory of that day when she'd climbed to the highest step of the ladder in the linen-room, reaching for a clean white gown. She'd been dreaming about Clive even as she stretched out her hand to the top shelf and toppled over...

Ugh! She put both hands to her stomach as she remembered the pain...the bleeding. And then there had been the stretcher, the trip to Theatre for the evacuation of uterus...the long days of depression when everyone had told her it was all for the best.

But she had known otherwise. She'd known that she would have been happy with Clive Hamilton, if only he hadn't been such a swine. If only he hadn't treated her like a one-night stand.

She could forgive him everything but that.

CHAPTER FOUR

THE maid had gone when Penny went back into her room. The curtains were drawn against the scorching rays of the sun and the air-conditioning had been turned up. She'd always thought there was something depressingly funereal about having the curtains drawn during the day. But she decided not to change them as she would probably be spending most of the day downstairs in the clinic.

She pulled the brand new uniform over her expensive lacy underwear. Fleetingly, she tried to remember why she'd lashed out on this hidden finery — Janet Reger pants and bra — horrendously expensive . . .but worth every penny in terms of restoring her confidence. Oh, yes, it had been the day after she'd got the letter from Victor telling her to apply for the job in Egypt. And she'd gone out to that little boutique in Knightsbridge and bought something to remind herself that she was still a young woman and not a nun.

She fastened the buttons of the white cotton blouse before pulling over the pale blue sleeveless tunic. Looking in the mirror, she decided it was quite an attractive outfit. She pinned on the white cap, pulling her long dark hair behind her neck and fixing it with a narrow ribbon. Maybe it would be easier to cope with if she bundled the whole lot under the cap?

But that made her look so severe. And she didn't want to look severe. She wanted to look approachable, attractive, desirable even.

'Desirable to whom?' she asked her reflection in the mirror. She smiled. 'No, don't answer that! Didn't I tell you a thousand times it's over?'

The day staff nurse was waiting for her when she went through the door of the clinic.

'Welcome, Sister Byrne. I am Staff Nurse Nadia.'

She was an amply proportioned woman of about thirty. Penny took the outstretched hand, feeling the strength and capability in the firm grip. She surmised that here was a nurse she would be able to rely on.

'I'm pleased to meet you, Nurse Nadia. I hope you're going to be able to show me the ropes.'

The Egyptian woman's eyes flickered momentarily. 'But you are in charge, Sister. I shall endeavour to serve you as best I can.'

Penny smiled. 'I may be in charge, but I'm still a stranger in your country. It's going to be some time before I get used to the routine and the different medical scenario. So we'll work together and pool our ideas for the good of the patients. . . OK?'

Nadia smiled, revealing strong pearly white teeth in her dark face. 'I shall endeavour to be of service, Sister.'

This polite servility was something Penny would have to get used to! But it was not unpleasant after the problems of coping with some of the young student nurses in London. Being one of the youngest sisters in the hospital, at only twenty-five, she had sometimes had to stick her neck out to enforce discipline where it was needed for the smooth running of the ward.

'Let's go and look at our emergency patient,' Penny said, quickly walking through the reception area. 'How is Mrs Greenwood this morning?'

'I have her charts here, Sister. Blood-pressure slightly raised, pulse regular, temperature normal. . .'

Nurse Nadia was reeling off the chart as they walked. Penny began to feel reassured about her patient. She pushed open the door of the private room and was even more delighted when she found Sarah Greenwood sitting up in bed, blonde hair combed back from her relaxed-looking face.

'My, what a difference! You look years younger,' Penny said, crossing over to the bed.

Automatically, she took hold of the patient's wrist and felt for the full, bounding pulse. She smiled down at her patient as she made her own careful check.

'I can't thank you enough, Sister,' Sarah Greenwood said. 'And James will add his thanks when he arrives.'

'When will that be?' Penny asked, remembering Clive's wish to have a talk with the husband.

'Some time this afternoon. Dr Hamilton sent him a fax last night to tell him what was happening. He phoned me this morning to say he would drive home as soon as he could. He had an important meeting but he said he would cancel it.'

Penny caught the intrinsic pride in Sarah's voice that her husband should find her predicament worthy of cancelling an important business meeting. And why not? she thought. It's his child as well as Sarah's. Men!

But she didn't voice her thoughts out loud. Her patient was obviously besotted with this young husband. Wasn't love a wonderful emotion? An unpredictable, nonsensical emotion, but nevertheless something which made the world go round.

'Dr Hamilton would like to have a chat with your husband this evening.'

'Why?' The patient's voice was instantly agitated. 'I'm going to be OK, aren't I? I'm not going to lose the baby, am I.'

Always give the patient the truth, said the professional voice inside Penny's head. Don't beat about the bush.

'It's too early to say, Sarah. We've taken you off the IV because it's not a good idea to prolong the treatment we gave you last night. But we'll have to keep you here for observation for a while to see if Mother Nature has any more tricks up her sleeve. I'm going to take you along to the treatment-room for a scan so I'll be in a better position to reassure you after that.'

Nurse Nadia brought in a wheelchair so that their patient wouldn't have any strain on her short trip to the treatment-room. Penny was impressed by the layout of this compact clinic. Every inch of space was used in a highly efficient manner. She hadn't yet had time to see the whole area, but she promised herself she would explore as soon as she had a spare minute, which didn't look like being until the end of the morning, judging by the number of people waiting in the glass-fronted waiting-room that led off from Reception.

They met Dr Fakry coming along from the medical staffroom. He smiled and greeted them with his usual courteous manner.

'Good morning, ladies. I'm going to start morning surgery. Do you think, Sister, that you could spare Staff Nurse Nadia for a while?'

Penny smiled back. 'But of course. I'll come along too when I've given Mrs Greenwood her scan.'

'Come along by all means, Sister, but I may not need your services today.' The tall Egyptian looked down at their patient. 'How are you feeling this morning, Mrs Greenwood?'

'Much better, Doctor. When can I go back upstairs to our hotel room?'

The dark Egyptian eyes gave nothing away. 'Mustn't rush things. We'll see what Dr Hamilton has to say when he gets back from Hurghada this evening.'

The scan was encouraging. Penny could see that no harm had come to the foetus during the uterine contractions. It was a good size, normal in every way and very active. She reassured Sarah Greenwood that all was well, but cautioned her to take things easy.

'We can't take any chances for the last few weeks. You'll have to rest all the time so that the contractions don't start up again.'

The patient's face clouded over. 'I can rest upstairs in my room. I hate being separated from my husband.'

'Wait until Dr Hamilton returns,' Penny said, hating herself for prevaricating but knowing that Clive wouldn't want her to make promises that couldn't be kept.

She wheeled Sarah back to her room and settled her comfortably in the bed before hurrying into the consulting-room.

Dr Fakry looked up from his desk. 'I can manage with Nurse Nadia helping me, Sister. Take the rest of the day off. You had a busy night, I believe. Perhaps you'd like to send the next patient in before you go.'

'Well, if you're sure,' Penny said, finding that she was warming even more to this Egyptian doctor.

'Of course I'm sure. You don't need to be here during the day unless we have an emergency. The nurses are very capable.'

Penny looked into the waiting-room and called in the next patient and then prepared to go off duty. She decided to take advantage of her spare time to look around the areas of the clinic she hadn't yet seen.

She started at the glass front of the building which gave her the impression of being in a goldfish bowl. The floor-length windows were totally revealing, but no treatment took place in the front rooms which housed the reception area and the waiting-room. Walking along the first corridor behind these highly visible areas, she came to the treatment-room and two consulting-rooms. Behind this technical area was the surgical unit, comprising a small operating-theatre, an ante-room and a recovery room which could be used as an intensive-care unit in an emergency.

Beyond the surgical unit there were six private rooms which looked out over the gardens. Clive had told her that it was rare to have all six rooms occupied. At the moment Sarah Greenwood was their only in-patient.

She wandered back along the corridor, feeling suddenly at a loose end. It was nice to be dismissed in the middle of the morning, but she had no idea how she was going to spend the day. There were so many things she wanted to do, but the long journey from England and the lack of sleep had taken their toll and she found herself unwilling to make the effort to go out and play the eager tourist. Another day, she promised herself, she would cross the Nile to see the Valley of the Kings or she would ride into Luxor town centre in a horse-drawn calèche or she would. . .but not today!

Today she would pamper herself, lie beside the pool and start her sun-tan, she decided as she walked through into the medical staffroom. This was a long area at the side of the clinic, looking out over gardens that led down to the edge of the Nile. A diminutive Egyptian auxiliary nurse relaxing in one of the comfortable armchairs leapt to her feet.

'Good morning, Sister. I am Nurse Saida. I came early to the clinic today. My duty starts at midday.'

Penny smiled reassuringly at the nervous young girl as she walked over to the windows that opened on to a veranda. 'I'm pleased to meet you, Nurse Saida.'

She was relieved to see that the nurse sat down again. This polite, almost military awareness of rank was unfamiliar and unnecessary. But she remembered she was in a foreign country and had a lot to learn.

She walked through the open French windows to admire the fabulous view. Standing for a few minutes on the veranda watching a white-sailed felucca drifting past, it seemed to her that the felucca's sails fluttering in the wind looked like butterflies' wings.

After a brief visit to her room she ensconced herself beside the swimming-pool, in her new white bikini, with a bottle of sun-tan lotion and the paperback she'd bought at Gatwick airport and started reading on the plane. She'd just got to the exciting bit and she was dying to see how it ended.

The sun was hotter than she'd anticipated. After only a few minutes she moved under one of the large umbrellas. So much for the sun-tan! Feeling sleepy, she decided to retreat to her room and return when the day had cooled down.

The cool peace of her room was like a sedative. She drifted off into a deep slumber and slept for most of the day, waking refreshed in the early evening. Drawing back the curtains, she saw that the sun was slanting in the sky. It was a perfect time for a twilight swim. She pulled on her new white Lycra bikini with the cut-away legs, covered it with a large cotton T-shirt, and went down in the lift.

It was sheer bliss to dive into the pool and feel the refreshing water on her hot skin. Mmm, this was the life! She surfaced and pulled the hair back from her face. The low sun was dazzling her eyes. For an instant she thought she was dreaming. She'd assumed that Clive would still be journeying back through the desert.

The halo of sunlight around the head of the approaching figure made him look like one of the Egyptian gods. His bronzed frame exuded virility, excitement, sensual promise. . .

She shuddered in the water and turned over on her back, trying to pretend she hadn't noticed him.

'I see you're taking things easy, Penny,' Clive drawled before diving into the pool, surfacing only inches away from her.

She ran a wet hand over her straggling hair.

'No, don't do that.' His fingers closed around the soaking strands that half covered her eyes and made it difficult to see. 'You look so young and vulnerable with your hair all mussed up. I remember. . .'

He stopped in mid-sentence and a secret, enigmatic smile crept over his rugged face. His fingers were still entwined in her hair.

Motionless, she held her breath, unwilling to break the magic spell that had descended on the pool with the twilight rays of the sun. They were the only people around. Everyone else had retired to their rooms to prepare for the evening ahead.

'What do you remember?' she asked in a hoarse voice.

His fingers in her hair became more demanding as he hooked his hand around the back of her neck. 'It's difficult to remember anything when you're looking so bewitching. When I came along the poolside just now you reminded me of a mermaid trying to escape from civilisation, striking out through the water until you were totally out of your depth.'

And then he kissed her. She could do nothing to stop him and her treacherous body responded with a tremulous urge to be close to him. Oh, she was out of her depth all right!

She was treading water as the delicious sensual waves of emotion rippled down her spine. His warm, demanding mouth was sending shivers over her wet skin. She moved her legs to keep afloat and their thighs touched beneath the water. His arms moved quickly to enclose her in his tantalising embrace.

'I'm sinking,' she whispered, not sure whether she was talking about her emotional turmoil or the physical impossibility of holding out against this man.

'I've got you,' he murmured, pulling her so close to him that she thought she would stop breathing.

Time stood still as she gave herself up to the heat of the moment. But through half-open eyes she caught sight of someone approaching the pool.

'Let me go, Clive.' With trembling hands she tried to push him away.

Reluctantly he relaxed his grip, running a hand through his dark, unruly hair.

'Always the prude,' he taunted her as she began to swim away from him.

'Not always,' she called back over her shoulder.

With swift strokes he was by her side. 'But why the change? What have I done to make you so bitter?'

She opened her mouth and swallowed some of the water. Spluttering with indignation at his insensitivity, she rounded on him. 'Wouldn't you be bitter if you'd been ignored for all these years?'

A puzzled frown crossed his face. 'But that was your choice, Penny, not mine.'

Now it was her turn to be puzzled. 'My choice, Clive?'

A shadow fell across the pool. Penny looked up to see a fair-haired young man in a well cut lightweight suit.

'Forgive me for intruding but I was told I might find Dr Hamilton here. Are you by any chance. . .?'

'I'm Dr Hamilton.' Clive was instantly the professional, hauling himself out of the pool and standing tall beside the stranger. 'How can I help you?'

'My name is James Greenwood. I believe you wanted to see me about my wife's condition.'

Penny watched and as the two men shook hands she decided it would be a good time to make her escape. She had no desire to be ogled in her bikini by her patient's husband. Far better he should meet her when she was in her protective uniform. And she had no desire to continue her conversation with

Clive. 'Her decision' indeed! She was frowning as she climbed out of the pool and wrapped her towel around her. She cast her mind back to that fateful evening five years ago. Had she said anything that might indicate she didn't want to see him again? Had she?

'Oh, Sister, just a moment!'

She stiffened and pulled the towel more closely around her as Clive sprinted around the edge of the pool.

'I've suggested eight o'clock in the clinic for a chat with James Greenwood. Can you make it?'

She hesitated.

His eyes flickered. 'I understand you haven't been overwhelmed with work today, so I would appreciate it if you could be present. Afterwards, I thought we could have dinner together.'

'You're very sure of yourself,' she said, in an ominously quiet voice. 'I'll come along for the professional consultation, but afterwards——'

'Afterwards we'll see what happens,' he cut in, a sardonic smile playing on his lips.

She turned and walked away with as much dignity as she could muster, considering the towel barely touched the top of her thighs. She felt as if Clive's eyes upon her were scorching her skin!

The clinic was quiet when she pushed her way through the glass doors and approached the reception desk. Nurse Samira raised her dark head from the letter she was typing and smiled.

'Dr Hamilton is in his consulting-room, Sister Byrne. You are to join him, I understand.'

'Is Mr Greenwood here?'

'Not yet, Sister, but he is expected any minute. Staff Nurse Rania is taking care of his wife. Perhaps you would like to meet the staff nurse? She was asking me about you when she came on duty at four o'clock.'

'I'll go along to Mrs Greenwood's room now,' Penny said.

'But please, do not keep Dr Hamilton waiting. He can be a very impatient man.'

Penny smiled. 'I do know that, Nurse Samira, but it's kind of you to remind me.'

The Egyptian nurse's eyes flickered and the corners of her mouth moved ever so slightly upwards. Penny had the distinct impression that the girl was observing her relationship with Clive with too much interest. It had been insane to allow herself to be carried away in the swimming-pool. As far as she knew there had been no one around, and the twilight sky above the palm trees had dimmed. But still, she must be more careful not to allow her heart to rule her head in future. Clive was certainly impatient, but he was also demanding. And if she gave in to his demands it would lead her nowhere except to another let-down.

She went quickly along to Sarah Greenwood's room. Staff Nurse Rania was settling their patient into bed. Penny introduced herself to the staff nurse, chatted to her patient, checked out the charts, and prescribed drugs before going along to the consulting-room. Before she left she had to satisfy her patient's curiosity about what was going to happen to her.

'Your husband is going to see Dr Hamilton this evening and we'll determine the best course of treatment, Sarah,' Penny told her patient gently. 'Leave it with me and I'll get back to you.'

The patient leaned back against her pillows. 'And James will come to see me when you've finished your talk, won't he?'

Penny patted Sarah's hand. 'Of course he will.'

The patient grasped Penny's hand and looked beseechingly at her. 'The trouble is, James is always so busy. He has so little time for me nowadays. I know I should have stayed back in England and let him come out on his own, but I was afraid. . .well, you know. . . I didn't want him to forget he was married.' She stopped, embarrassed. 'I shouldn't have said that. It sounds disloyal.'

Penny gave her a reassuring smile. 'It's not disloyal, Sarah. It's sound common sense. I'm sure when your husband realises how much you need him at this difficult time he'll spend more time with you.'

Sarah brightened visibly, but didn't look totally convinced.

Penny found the two men deep in conversation in the consulting-room. Clive looked up and his eyes held a tender expression as she walked in.

'This is Sister Byrne, our sister in charge of the clinic; this is James Greenwood,' Clive said, unnecessarily.

Penny avoided eye contact with their patient's husband, but the tall young man moved forward to grasp her by the hand.

'I do believe you look even more fetching in your uniform than in your bikini, Sister,' James Greenwood said in a blatantly seductive voice.

Oh, no! Penny thought as she removed her hand from the eager grasp. Not another man who thinks he's the answer to every maiden's prayer. She moved away quickly to align herself with Clive and settle in a chair beside his desk.

'I've been speaking to your wife this evening, Mr Greenwood——' she began.

'Oh, please, call me James. . .'

'And I'm a little worried about her mental state. She needs to be reassured that all is well between you. So might I suggest that you give her all the time and attention you can possibly manage? She's had a rough time recently and——'

'Don't worry your pretty little head, Sister,' James Greenwood broke in, seeminly unaware of Penny's disapproval. 'I've been shopping in Luxor this evening and bought the most beautiful necklace. Sarah will love it.'

'I'm not talking about bringing your wife presents, Mr Greenwood. I'm talking about giving her some of your time. For some unknown reason which maybe you could explain she has the distinct impression that you might just take off and leave her to have this baby all by herself. She actually told me that she'd got herself into a state of anxiety when you went up to Aswan and that was when the premature contractions came on. She's a very sensitive woman and needs constant reassurance. Sometimes mental anxiety can produce physical symptoms.'

James Greenwood leaned back in his armchair and drew in his breath.

'What else did she tell you, Sister?'

'She told me about her previous marriage. I can understand why she might feel insecure, especially in view of the fact. . .' She paused, realising that she'd talked herself into a corner.

The young husband smiled. 'In view of the fact that I'm ten years younger than she is. But women are like good wine; they improve with age.'

Clive, who had been listening intently to the interchange between Penny and James Greenwood, now leaned forward. 'I know that and you know that, but have you told your wife?'

James Greenwood tossed back his head and gave a hoarse laugh. 'Of course I have. . .millions of times, but Sarah still feels insecure. Her first husband was a swine. She was still suffering from the effects of being jilted when she met me. I helped to put the pieces together. Now don't you two worry about me; I'll do all I can to keep the little woman happy. Incidentally, what are the baby's chances?'

'Fifty-fifty,' Clive replied in a grim tone. 'Given ideal conditions, the baby stands a good chance. But if Sarah starts worrying or the contractions come on again before the baby is ready to face the world it could be a very difficult labour and an unpredictable outcome.'

James Greenwood stood up. Clive's grave words

seemed to have barely touched him. 'Well, thanks a lot, Doc.' He nodded briefly towards Penny, seemingly aware that she wasn't the easy-going dolly-bird he'd first taken her for. 'Thanks, Sister.'

He turned at the door. 'Oh, just one more thing; I presume you'll be keeping my wife in the clinic for a while. Don't worry about the expense. The company will pay. Just do everything you have to.'

'Are you going to visit your wife now?' Penny said quickly.

James Greenwood glanced at his watch and frowned. 'Hell's bells, is that the time? I can give her ten minutes and then I'll have to shoot off.' He glanced from Clive to Penny and added, 'An important client has asked me out to dinner. There's no relaxing in this job. Pity Sarah can't understand that.'

'What job is that, Mr Greenwood?' Clive asked with icy calm.

'Export-import, Doc. Takes me all over the world. Must dash.'

As the door closed, Penny looked at Clive. 'What an obnoxious man, full of his own importance; he's absolutely no sympathy for his wife. Some women attract the wrong men and Sarah must be one of them. To get one swine of a husband must be bad enough, but then to marry another. . .'

She broke off, aware of the anxiety etched on Clive's face.

He took a deep breath. 'Sarah thinks James is wonderful. She doesn't know he's two-timing her.'

'What makes you think that?'

'There's a certain young lady waiting in the foyer at this very moment and she doesn't look like an important business client to me. They were sitting at one of the corner tables behind those large potted palms. I only saw them quite by chance as I went to Reception for my key. She was obviously more than a passing acquaintance.'

'The beast!' Penny said vehemently.

'I couldn't agree more. But then, some men are like that.'

Penny's patience snapped. 'It takes one to know one.'

A deep frown appeared on Clive's handsome face. 'I didn't know you had such a low opinion of me. In the circumstances it's probably just as well that I can't take you out to dinner this evening.'

Penny faced him with blazing eyes. 'Don't tell me you have a prior engagement with an important business client.'

He gave her a sardonic smile. 'I could say that, but it wouldn't be true. No, the truth is that I've had a phone call from the sister in charge of the Hurghada clinic where I spent the day. The problem I went to resolve is still there, so I'll have to go back again. . .tonight.'

'Tonight?' she echoed. 'But couldn't it wait until morning? Isn't it rather dangerous driving across the desert at night?'

He smiled. 'I've done it before. . .but your concern is touching. If I didn't know you better I'd think you were disappointed at losing me. Incidentally,

Ahmed Fakry will be in charge again, but I'll keep in touch by phone.'

'How long will you be away?' She tried to sound as if it were purely a professional query, but the pathos in her voice gave her away.

He moved closer. 'About a month. Hopefully I should have sorted things out by then. Goodbye, Penny.'

He dropped a kiss on the side of her cheek before heading for the door and moving swiftly out into the corridor. She ran her hand across the skin where he had kissed her. A month was going to seem an awfully long time.

CHAPTER FIVE

For the first week Penny kept herself busy with her clinic work and told herself that she wasn't missing Clive in the least. But alone at night in her luxurious room she knew she was kidding herself. Coming out to Egypt and meeting Clive again had opened up an old wound that was going to be difficult to heal. It had been difficult enough the first time, but second time around it was going to be well nigh impossible.

She insisted on helping Ahmed Fakry and the staff nurses with the morning surgeries so as to keep herself fully occupied. There had been a recent epidemic of gastroenteritis which had affected many of the tourists, and she was called out sometimes in the middle of the night to begin medication and reassure the hotel guests that they only felt as if they were going to die, but that they would recover in a matter of days. She also had to make clinically sure that her diagnoses were correct and this entailed a certain amount of liaising with the hospital, which had a well equipped path. lab.

After a week had passed she was beginning to feel thoroughly at home with her medical duties. She went down into the clinic, greeting Nurse Samira, who was now on days, with a cheery smile.

'Good morning, Samira. Any messages?'

Samira shook her head and Penny felt the customary disappointment which she nevertheless hid behind her bright smile.

'We've got a new patient arrived this morning, Sister. I didn't call you because it didn't seem like an emergency. He got here about an hour ago. I've given him some breakfast. Poor soul, he's absolutely starving.'

'Has Dr Fakry seen him?'

'I didn't want to get him in either. I knew I could deal with this myself, Sister.'

'But what's the matter with the patient? You really should get a diagnosis before you start treating a patient, Samira.'

Samira shrugged. 'But there was no need. It's obvious he's suffering from exhaustion and malnutrition. . .nothing that a few days' rest and good food won't put right. He's walked all the way over from Hurghada to see Dr Hamilton.'

Penny frowned. 'But Dr Hamilton is over in Hurghada.'

'He didn't know that. Poor boy, it took him a week to walk over, Sister. Mohammed is only fifteen and he hasn't even got shoes. The desert can get pretty hot during the day and it's nearly two hundred miles. As far as I can make out he must have set off the day that Dr Hamilton went back to Hurghada. They must have passed each other somewhere along the way.'

'Well, where have you put this Mohammed?'

'Room two. . .next to Mrs Greenwood. She's been in and out of his room looking after him. I think she likes playing at mother.'

'She's supposed to be resting. I hope she hasn't been doing too much.'

'Oh, no; she's only been talking to him and making sure he eats his breakfast. And that wasn't difficult. He wolfed it down in no time.'

Penny was intrigued. To walk nearly two hundred miles the fifteen-year-old Mohammed must have a fairly pressing need to see Clive!

She found the young boy leaning back against crisp white cotton pillowcases, an empty tray beside his bed. His deeply sunken eyes held a haunted look and his fingers, clutching and curling at the end of the sheet, tapered off to black, grimy fingernails bitten down to the skin. She noticed with concern that he was thin to the point of emaciation.

'Mohammed, I'm Sister Byrne. I'm told you've walked a long way. How are you feeling now?'

'Tired. I want to sleep before you send me back. Let me stay till I feel stronger.'

Penny sat down on the edge of the bed and took the young boy's hand. 'You can most certainly stay, Mohammed. I wouldn't dream of sending you away. But what made you come trekking across the desert to see Dr Hamilton? Did Nurse Samira tell you he's gone over to Hurghada?'

The boy nodded miserably. 'I wanted to see if he would give me a job. He's such a nice man. I knew I could trust him when I saw him a week ago. I went to the clinic to get some medicine for my sister and he was very kind to me. So I thought I would try to get a job at his clinic. I had no money so I walked here only to find I should have stayed over at Hurghada if I'd wanted to see him.'

'But what kind of job do you want, Mohammed?' Penny asked carefully, trying not to dampen the boy's spirits any further.

The thin shoulders beneath the oversized clinic gown shrugged. 'I will do anything...anything. I have no work at home apart from helping my family and that's women's work. It's not good for a man to have to wash dishes and spread the clothes out in the sun. I want a real job...a man's job. I don't mind starting at the bottom. I'll sweep the floors, empty the rubbish bins...anything...until I'm old enough to become a doctor.'

'A doctor?' Penny quickly changed her incredulous tone. 'Well, it's a very worthwhile profession. I'm sure Dr Hamilton would be interested to hear about your ambition. Unfortunately, he's not here and I don't think he'll be back for another three weeks or so.'

'I will rest awhile and then I'll return to Hurghada to see him,' said the boy in a grave, determined voice.

'I think you'll need to spend some time recovering, Mohammed. Why not stay here with us until Dr Hamilton returns?'

She knew she was sticking her neck out, but there was something about the boy that appealed to her and she was loath to see him wander back across the desert again only to arrive at the other side in the same appalling condition.

The boy's face brightened. 'You are very kind,

Sister. I would like to stay. . .but only if I can work. Give me work, please.'

'When you're stronger I'll find you some work.' She reached down and took hold of the cloth bound around his forearm. This was certainly no professional bandage. 'What did you do here?'

'It is nothing. Nurse Samira wanted to take it off when I went into the shower, but I told her it was better to leave it like this. It will hurt if you remove it.'

'Well, I'll just take a little peep. . .like this.' Carefully Penny removed the makeshift bandage to reveal a long, deep cut. It didn't take an expert to see that this would require suturing.

'What happened?'

Mohammed hesitated. 'I was in a fight. Someone pulled a knife on me.'

'Why were you fighting?'

The boy passed a hand over his face as if the memory irritated it. 'I had some money in a leather purse, hidden beneath my robes. Not much, but enough to buy bread until I could get work here at the clinic. One night as I slept beside the road, curled up in my blanket, a man drove up on a motorbike. He stopped. I thought he was going to give me a lift, but he leaned over me and told me to give him all the money I had. I tried to push him away but he was too strong for me. And then he pulled out a knife and cut my arm as I struggled. He drove off into the night after stealing my purse.'

'Oh, you poor boy.' Penny was examining the wound more carefully. 'It's a bad cut; it's going to need some stitches. I'll get a wheelchair and take you along to the treatment-room.'

'No need for a wheelchair. I'm not an invalid.' Mohammed stood proudly upright, his thin legs wobbling only slightly with the exertion.

Penny smiled. 'Come along, then, but catch hold of my arm if you start to feel faint.'

In the treatment-room she settled Mohammed on the couch and carefully cleansed the wound with antiseptic. It was a deep cut but it was clean. The boy's innate good health had saved him from infection, but she decided to give him an anti-tetanus injection to be on the safe side.

'Now, it's back to bed for you, my boy. Rest and good food is what you need for a few days and when you're strong enough I'll find you a job.'

During the next three weeks, Penny was delighted to see the progress Mohammed made. He had a voracious appetite and she took pleasure in watching the emaciated body filling out. After two weeks he was fit to start light cleaning duties, and Penny could see by the way he approached his menial tasks that he was a good worker.

But would he make a doctor? She knew very little about his academic ability. It would seem that he was wishing for the moon.

A month had passed since Clive had gone to Hurghada. They'd spoken briefly on the phone under strained professional conditions on a couple of occasions, but there had been no personal conversation. And he gave no indication of why he'd gone back so suddenly. Sometimes she wondered if he'd invented the emergency to escape from her. Perhaps his conscience pricked him about the way he'd treated her and he couldn't stand the constant reminder.

She flicked a clean cover on to the couch in the treatment-room one morning at the end of surgery and allowed her thoughts to dwell momentarily on Clive. She was trying desperately to get him out of her system again. She wasn't plagued nearly so much with broken nights. In fact she'd slept like a log the previous evening——

'Telephone for you, Sister.'

Staff Nurse Nadia's husky voice cut through her thoughts. The tall, amply proportioned young woman was grinning from ear to ear.

'It's Dr Hamilton. He wants me to take over from you. They're sending a staff nurse from the hospital to do my work and I'm to be acting sister.'

Penny felt her stomach lurch. Clive was going to get rid of her! He was sending her back to England. And she didn't want to go. She really didn't! She wanted——

'Dr Hamilton is waiting on the phone, Sister,' Nurse Nadia urged.

'Fine!' Penny realised that she'd been rooted to the spot as her emotions performed a Highland fling. She glanced across at the wall phone, unwilling to take the devastating news in front of the elated staff nurse. 'That will be all, Nurse Nadia. You can go back to your duties.'

She wanted the smile disappear from the staff

nurse's face as she hurried away. This was the first time Penny had pulled rank on the staff nurse, but she felt entitled to in the circumstances. And why had the woman been so callous as to stand there looking like the cat that had licked the cream? She unhooked the phone from the wall.

'Clive! How nice of you to call.' She would go down with all guns blazing! He needn't think she was going to be a push-over. 'How can I help you?'

'Has Nurse Nadia broken the news to you, Penny?'

'She has indeed.'

Silence. . .then, 'Well, how soon can you get over here?'

'Get over where?' Penny echoed. 'What are you talking about? I thought you were. . . Nurse Nadia said she was taking over from me and——'

'So she is.' Clive's voice barely concealed his impatience. 'I've arranged that she will take over because I want you to come over to Hurghada. . . Penny, are you still there?'

'Yes, I'm still here. You mean you want me to work over there?'

'Of course, what else?'

What else indeed! Her pulses were racing. 'Well, it's all rather sudden, but if you give me a couple of days to tie things up here I'll be with you. How do I get there?'

'Take a taxi; we'll pay at this end. Look, I've got to go now, so——'

'Clive, just a moment! Two things; firstly, I'm not happy about Sarah Greenwood. You were quite right when you said that her husband is two-timing her. I saw him with a young woman. They were setting off in a calèche to go to Luxor. He doesn't even try to be discreet.'

'Does Sarah know anything about this?'

'Of course not. We're keeping her resting in her room. Ahmed Fakry is very sympathetic to the situation and refuses to let her go back to her hotel room until the baby is born.'

'Quite right. Well, you must make sure that Nurse Nadia knows that Sarah must be shielded from all strain. That's all we can do. It's no good appealing to James Greenwood's better nature. I don't think he has one. They can sort out their marriage problems after this baby is safely delivered.' He paused as if to compose his feelings again. It was obvious to Penny, even over the phone, that Clive had no sympathy with the errant husband. She refrained from making any adverse comments on this occasion.

'And the second problem is the young Mohammed I told you about. He's still got this bee in his bonnet about becoming a doctor and——'

'Bring him with you in the taxi. His family live over here. We'll sort something out. I'll expect you on Thursday. Travel early before the sun is too hot. Leave at seven and you'll be here before lunch. Goodbye, Penny. Have a pleasant journey.'

The line went dead, leaving her with a feeling that she hadn't resolved half the problems she wanted to. But she would have time to talk to Clive when she got over to Hurghada. She would have time to be with him.

She'd forgotten to ask how long she would be staying over there on the Red Sea. But it didn't matter. The fact that she was actually going was enough for her. The enforced separation from Clive had told her one thing—that she was still in love with him, that she always would be. And she simply had to find out what had happened to him in the intervening years, and why he hadn't contacted her.

She remembered his puzzled voice by the swimming-pool a month ago when she'd challenged him about not making contact.

'That was your choice, Penny,' he'd said.

She gave a deep sigh as she cast her mind back to that wonderful evening five years ago. What had she actually said to him when he'd promised to contact her?

They had been lying amid the crumpled sheets of the wide king-sized bed and she'd never felt so happy in her whole life. Clive had just cracked open a bottle of champagne and she'd snuggled up against his hard, muscular chest, trying not to spill her glass but unwilling to sit up and spoil the precious moment of togetherness. The room seemed to be bathed in a heavenly aura of unreality.

And Clive had said that he must see her again, that he was never going to let her disappear from his life. The only problem had been his impending trip to West Africa. He was to be flown straight out to the north of Matala to set up a new air-doctor service in the bush. She must be sure not to forget to write down the address of her flat in Battersea and the phone number.

'You do want to see me again, don't you, Penny?'

Over the years the sound of that haunting, husky voice drifted back into her consciousness.

She searched her memory for the exact reply she'd made. It had been a muffled 'Yes, oh, yes', and then, as his lips had swooped down on hers, the champagne had spilled on the sheets and they were making love again.

How could he have misinterpreted her reply? How could he say that it was her decision not to make contact again? She'd written her address and phone number in his diary at his insistence before she'd left. Would she have done that if she'd wanted to forget him?

Perhaps he'd lost his diary and didn't want to admit it. That was what she would like to believe most. But then he could have phoned the hospital and made contact with her there. No, the plain fact of the matter was that he'd forgotten all about her until she'd turned up in Egypt five weeks ago and now he was trying to make a plausible story, hoping she would have only a hazy recollection of what had been said.

But at the very least she was going to find out what he'd been up to during the past five years. Even if the truth hurt.

CHAPTER SIX

PENNY was trying not to be too impatient as the ancient taxi chugged its way through the desert. Clouds of sandy dust blew up around them. It had been bad luck to find that the car she'd hired was one of the many taxis that didn't have air-conditioning and so they were forced to drive with the windows down to get some air.

Mohammed was restless too. Penny could tell that he wasn't looking forward to returning to his home village. He was obviously anxious about how his parents would deal with him for having run away from home.

The bleak landscape made Penny feel as if they'd landed on the moon, but the harsh, hostile contours softened as they drove down towards the Red Sea. Penny felt her spirits rising and her thoughts turned again to Clive. He was rarely absent from them now. And she was going to see him. . .in a very short time.

She looked out across the blue water.

'Do you know why they call it the Red Sea?' she asked Mohammed.

The young boy smiled, revealing strong pearly white teeth. 'Because when the sun sets over those mountains the sea soaks up the bright golden glow. The Red Sea is very beautiful at sunset.'

'It's very beautiful by day too,' Penny said. 'I think I'm going to enjoy working over here.'

'I hope you will stay, Sister,' the boy said shyly. 'And please, when I first meet my mother, don't leave me alone with her. She will be very angry with me.'

Penny gave Mohammed a reassuring smile. 'We'll all do what we can to help you. I know Dr Hamilton will want to smooth things out with your family.'

The boy brightened visibly. 'I'm looking forward to seeing Dr Hamilton again.'

Penny drew in her breath. So was she, but she was intensely nervous!

Clive was waiting for them in the reception area of the Red Sea Hotel. As their taxi drew up into the forecourt he came out into the bright midday sunlight. Penny's initial glance took in the sleek casual trousers, the white polo shirt open at the neck to reveal the dark hairs on his tanned chest. Her pulses began to race and she knew that nothing this man could do would make her dislike him. He was like a magnet drawing her towards him, and she would go willingly.

He hurried to open the car door for her and she climbed out as gracefully as she could. He took hold of her hands. They were both aware of prying eyes, but some of their previous caution had been removed by the month-long separation.

'I've missed you, Penny,' he said in a low, husky voice that only she could hear.

'Have you?' She felt as if she were in a dream as

she looked up into his eyes. 'Absence makes the heart grow fonder.'

His broad, sensual mouth curved into a sexy smile. 'It certainly does. You promised to have dinner with me a month ago, remember?'

Her heart started to thump madly. 'I remember . . .but I thought you might have forgotten.'

'Why should I forget something so important?'

'You found it very easy to forget me before I arrived out here in Egypt,' she said quietly.

He frowned, but remained looking down into her eyes, his fingers tightening over hers. When he spoke his voice was harsh, barely concealing his anger. 'How dare you claim I neglected you when it was you who. . .?'

He broke off, aware of Mohammed approaching them after carrying Penny's case into the hotel. Through clenched teeth he muttered, 'You and I have got to have a talk just as soon as we possibly can. Let's make it an evening when we're alone.' He relinquished her hands and turned to Mohammed.

'Good to see you again, Mohammed. I hear you've been earning your keep over at Luxor.'

The boy smiled. 'Sister allowed me to help out at the clinic. Nothing very difficult. But it will all be good experience for when I become a doctor.'

'There's more to being a doctor than practical work,' Clive said in a kindly voice. 'You'll have to work hard at your science subjects if you want to make the grade for medical school. So the first thing we have to do is get you back to school.'

The boy's face fell. 'But I can't go back to school.

The head teacher will kill me...if my mother hasn't killed me first.'

Clive reached out his hand and put it on the boy's shoulder. 'You'll have to face up to them like a man, Mohammed. That will be a good experience you can use in your medical training...doing something you don't want to do, something that makes you feel scared. Think of it as a positive step towards your final goal. I'm telling you, without this first step you'll get nowhere. No medical school will take you without the correct qualifications.'

For an instant, the boy looked sulky, as if he was about to run away again. Suddenly, he squared his shoulders and pulled himself to his full height. Clive still towered above him, but Penny could see that Mohammed was already modelling himself on his hero.

'OK, I'll go back home...but do you think you two could come with me? And can I still have a job with you, say, at the weekends, just to give me the experience?'

Clive ruffled Mohammed's hair. 'Come and have some lunch with us and then we'll all go to face your mother together. And I'll find you something to do at the weekend so long as it doesn't interfere with your homework.'

'Thanks a lot!' The boy's eyes were shining as they all went in through the main door.

The Red Sea Hotel was much smaller than the Nile Hotel, but Penny found it had a more personal, friendly feeling about it. The young man on the reception counter handed over the keys to her room and said he hoped she would enjoy staying with them.

'Come and have lunch before you go to your room,' Clive said, putting a hand under her arm. 'The dining-room is down those steps.'

He escorted her outside and down carpeted steps under the hot sun before reaching the pleasantly cool dining-room where ceiling fans whirred above their heads. Mohammed hung back as they reached the swing-door of the dining-room and asked where he was to have his lunch.

'In here with us, of course,' Clive replied, urging the suddenly shy young boy forwards.

The small dining-room was well staffed with white-coated waiters. They were ushered to a table with a splendid view of the gardens that led down to the sea, which was clearly visible in the noon sunshine.

Penny chose to have the *mourgan*, which was red mullet and reputed to have been caught in the sea that morning. The delicious taste seemed to bear out the authenticity of the waiter's claim. Mohammed, after initially being somewhat overawed at being seated on the medical-staff table, with its crisp white cloth and large, impeccably starched napkins, became decidedly loquacious and didn't stop asking questions throughout the whole of the meal, from starters to pudding.

Penny welcomed Mohammed's chatter because it allowed her to enjoy being with Clive without having to worry about the state of their relationship. This evening all would be revealed, and she wasn't sure she wanted to learn the truth. It might put an end to their new romance before it had started.

Breaking through Mohammed's eager questions, Clive introduced Penny to the other members of staff. There were two staff nurses, Hannan and Aziza, and two auxiliary nurses, Samia and Sona.

'Where is the clinic doctor?' Penny asked.

Clive's eyes flickered. 'We have to appoint another doctor. This was the problem I had to sort out.'

Penny was aware that the four young Egyptian nurses were leaning forward to catch the doctor's words, and she divined at once that Clive didn't want to discuss it at the table.

It wasn't until they were alone in the clinic consulting-room after lunch that she was able to broach the subject again. Mohammed had been taken on a tour of the gardens by one of the reception staff, so there was no one to overhear what was said.

'So what's the big mystery about the doctor, Clive?'

Clive leaned back in his chair and Penny settled herself in a chair at the other side of the desk. They had finished their brief tour of the clinic and she'd discovered that the facilities were much simpler over here. There was merely a consulting-room, a large treatment-room which could double as an emergency operating-theatre, and three private rooms for in-patients, so they'd been able to inspect the whole medical area very quickly.

Clive drew in his breath as he faced her across the

desk. The room was quiet with the calm of the afternoon siesta and his voice was crisp and clear.

'We've tried to hush up the scandal, but the Press will soon hear about it, I expect. You see, I discovered that the doctor appointed from England had forged qualifications. It turned out he'd dropped out of medical school after a couple of years and then gone to work as a medical orderly in the Far East. He'd kept moving from country to country so it was difficult to verify his track record.'

'But didn't anyone suspect he was a phoney when he started work here?'

Clive shook his head. 'To give him his due, he worked very hard and was totally convincing. The medical work here in Hurghada is rarely complicated so there was nothing he couldn't handle. But about a month ago when I was talking to him, he made a chance remark that set me thinking. I questioned him further on the medical case we were discussing and realised that we might have a rotten apple in the barrel. I think he knew I was on to him. I hoped I was wrong, but I made a few phone calls and waited for replies. When I got back to Luxor I received the call that confirmed my suspicions, so I came back at once. I had to report the matter to our people in London, and our bogus doctor was recalled to face the music. In the meantime I also realised that our sister in charge was in love with him and had been covering up as much as she could. So I had to ask her to leave last week. That was when I phoned you.'

'You've had a difficult time,' Penny observed in a quiet tone.

'I hated having to hand our young doctor over. But it was his own fault. He could have made the grade quite easily if he'd stuck to his studies. But now his career is in ruins and he'll never be trusted again. What a waste! We must make sure that Mohammed knows he's got to work hard and not give up at the first hurdle. . .talking of which, we ought to be getting on our way. The longer we leave it, the harder it will be to face Mohammed's mother.'

'Shall I put my uniform on to make the visit seem more official?' Penny asked.

Clive stood up and came around the desk. He put out his hand and took hold of the ends of her dark hair. 'Stay just as you are. Uniforms sometimes frighten people. I think Mohammed's mother will prefer to have a motherly chat with an approachable young woman like you. . . By the way, I like the sun-tan. It suits you.'

She blushed beneath the light colour that had been so difficult to acquire. By dint of getting up early and spending a few minutes each day in the less harmful morning rays she had slowly found her skin changing to an attractive shade. And she'd made sure that the white polo shirt she'd teamed with her cream linen trousers that day showed off her bare arms to good effect.

'I'm glad you approve,' she said quietly.

He bent his head and kissed her gently on the lips. 'I do indeed.'

He raised his head, but remained looking down at her with a quizzical look.

'What an enigma you are, Penny. You make life so difficult for yourself. If only——'

There was a light tapping on the door and Mohammed walked in without waiting for a reply.

'I'm as ready as I'll ever be to face my mother,' he announced with a cheery grin on his face. 'So let's go before my confidence vanishes again.'

Clive drove them along the side of the sea in his Land Rover until they reached a small group of mud-brick houses on higher ground about half a mile from the sea. Penny was struck by the stark simplicity of the dwellings. Mohammed's house was no more than a flimsy shack surrounded by a well beaten area of sandy soil where a few hens scratched hopefully.

The sound of their engine brought Mohammed's mother to the door. She was dressed completely in black cotton robes. Her gnarled features registered surprise when she saw her visitors, but she reached out her work-worn brown hand and placed it on her son's shoulder.

Penny couldn't understand what mother and son were saying, but it was obvious that Mohammed was being forgiven. The tears ran down the Egyptian woman's face as she poured out a torrent of words, at first in a scolding tone and then in a much gentler voice.

'My mother says would you like to come in the house? She is caring for my sister Mona and she cannot leave her, but she would like to offer you some refreshment.'

'Is your sister sick?' Clive asked quickly.

'No, not sick, she is with child and her time has come,' Mohammed replied easily. 'Come inside, please.'

They went through into the main living-room. It seemed dark after the bright sunshine and Penny's eyes took several seconds to become adjusted. The floor was a continuation of the outside earth but had been beaten down hard over the years. A couple of brightly coloured rugs eased the stark simplicity. There was a rough table surrounded by several wooden chairs and boxes.

Penny was about to sit down when an agonised call came from the next room. The mother hurried away.

'My sister,' Mohammed explained in a matter-of-fact tone as if it were perfectly natural for someone to cry out in agony. 'I will get your drinks because my mother has to——'

'Never mind the drinks!' Clive cut in briskly. 'Is your sister going to have any medical help with this baby?'

'My mother is the village midwife,' Mohammed replied proudly. 'We do not need medical help for a baby.'

'But is your mother qualified?' Clive asked.

Mohammed looked hurt. 'My mother has delivered so many babies she has lost count. This is my sister's third baby. There will be no problem otherwise——'

The young boy broke off as his mother reappeared, an anxious look on her face. She spoke rapidly to her son.

'My mother wishes you to help her, Doctor. There is a problem.'

Clive had already been able to translate what the mother was saying. He put his hand under Penny's arm and pulled her with him as they went through into the inner room.

Mohammed's sister, Mona, was lying on a low wooden bed; her face was wet with sweat and her eyes frightened as she looked up beseechingly.

'Help me, Doctor,' she muttered. 'All is not well with this baby. It is not as the others were. My mother, she tries, but I do not think she can help me.'

Clive went down on his knees beside the bed and made a brief but thorough examination. His face was grim as he turned to look at Penny.

'The umbilical cord is prolapsed,' he whispered. Then, turning back to the patient, he explained that he was going to take her immediately to the clinic.

Penny felt a *frisson* of fear running down her spine. She only hoped they would be in time. Once before she had helped to deliver a baby when the cord had prolapsed, and the birth had been successful. But that had been in a London teaching hospital and no time had been lost.

In her mind she quickly reviewed the situation. She knew that a prolapse of the cord occurred when the membranes ruptured and, as the waters rushed out, the cord was swept down past the presenting part of the foetus. The cord became compressed between the foetal head and the mother's pelvis, constituting a serious emergency, because the foetus would die from asphyxia unless delivered quickly. If the cervix was fully dilated, forceps could be applied, but as Mohammed's sister was still in the first stage of labour only an immediate Caesarean could save the baby.

The road back to the clinic seemed endless to Penny. The whole journey only took a few minutes, but she was petrified that they would be too late to save the baby. She sat on the back seat of the Land Rover, cradling the patient's head in her hands while Clive drove speedily around the narrow bends. She was sure that if they'd had any kind of medical equipment with them Clive would have attempted an emergency operation back in Mohammed's house. But, because they were merely on a social call and hadn't anticipated an emergency arising, neither of them had come prepared.

A trolley was found as soon as they reached the Red Sea Hotel, and they wheeled their patient into the treatment-room. Clive administered a general anaesthetic and Penny's relief as their patient went under was equal to that of the patient at being put into a state of oblivion.

'Scalpel, Sister.'

Penny handed over the sterile knife, thinking that this was the quickest emergency operation she'd handled. Only minimum sterile precautions had been possible due to the necessity for speed of action. She had barely had time to swab down the patient's abdomen before Clive's scalpel started the life-saving operation.

She watched as he made an incision in the lower segment of the uterus. The foetus was immediately obvious. She reached forward and helped Clive to deliver it through the abdominal wall.

A gasp of relief went up from the four nurses clustered around the table. They had all insisted on quickly scrubbing up as soon as they heard of the emergency, and Penny realised that they had assembled a good medical team here at Hurghada.

As Clive handed the tiny infant to Penny it gave a weak cry and the little hands moved up towards the crumpled features.

'It's a boy!' Staff Nurse Aziza called out happily. 'Mona will be delighted to have a son. I've known Mona and her husband since we were all at school together.'

Penny's eyes met Clive's above the mask and she could see he was smiling with relief. It had been touch-and-go. No one knew that better than they did. She wondered fleetingly what would have happened if they hadn't gone over to Mohammed's house.

Wrapping the tiny baby in a dressing towel, she began to cleanse his nostrils. Suddenly, Clive's hand was on her arm and he was whispering into her ear.

'We will have that dinner tonight, Penny. Even if I have to bring in extra staff from the hospital to help out here.'

She looked up into his eyes and saw the tender expression that she loved so much. Her pulses raced at the prospect of being with him. . .but she was still apprehensive about finding out the truth.

CHAPTER SEVEN

IT WAS nine o'clock before Penny and Clive were able to leave the clinic. Mona and her new baby had been settled in one of the private rooms. Penny was relieved to find that there were no complications after the baby had been delivered. Clive had sutured the clean abdominal wound and announced that the young mother was now as good as new again.

And indeed, when Mona had come round from the anaesthetic she had been remarkably fit. Her joy at discovering she had a son had been wonderful to witness. And she had insisted on breast-feeding the tiny infant as soon as possible. Penny had helped the young mother to lie on her side so that the weight of the baby cradled in her arms would fall on to the bed and not cause her any strain as she fed him.

The young husband had arrived, followed shortly afterwards by Mohammed with his parents. They had all wanted to stay on longer, but Clive had persuaded them that it was better for Mona to have some rest. The entire family had reluctantly departed, promising to return in the morning. Mohammed's mother had hung behind for a few minutes to thank Clive and Penny for saving the baby. She explained that she'd only ever witnessed that complication once before and on that occasion, to her intense sadness, the baby had died because she'd had no technological equipment.

Penny had felt her stomach lurch as she'd realised once more that, but for their intervention, the outcome would have been tragic. And now, driving away from the Red Sea Hotel, she had a feeling of intense satisfaction with her day. It had been a stroke of luck that she and Clive had been in Mona's mud-brick house at that precise moment. And it had been even more wonderful that they had been able to set up the Caesarean section so quickly.

She glanced sideways at Clive's profile outlined in the moonlight that was shining in through the car windows. She thought again how handsome he was . . .how strong and virile he looked. . .how she was hopelessly hooked on him even though she knew it didn't make sense. And she longed to know the truth as soon as possible. . .even if it shattered their romance. Because it was better she should find out now than later, when she'd succumbed again to his charismatic charms.

'You're very quiet,' Clive said and, as if sensing that she was watching him, he took his eyes from the sandy road for an instant and gave her a knowing look, as if reading her thoughts.

'I was thinking how good it is to relax,' she lied. 'It's been a long day.'

He was staring ahead at the road again, but he took one hand from the wheel and reached for hers. 'It was good having you with me today, Penny. I think we're going to make a great team.'

She swallowed. 'I hope so. . . I certainly hope so.'

His fingers tightened around hers. 'No doubt about it. Now relax and stop thinking about work. We're going out to enjoy ourselves. I'm taking you to my favourite restaurant and I think you'll love it.'

Abdou's Restaurant was on a peninsula of sandy ground that jutted out into the Red Sea. Abdou himself, a tall, prepossessing middle-aged Egyptian with the well padded flesh of the bon viveur, met them at the door and ushered them inside to a table by the window overlooking the sea. Large handwritten menus were presented and a bottle of ice-cold champagne uncorked.

Penny smiled at Clive across the top of her bubbles as they raised their glasses.

'To our new-found partnership,' Clive said as their glasses touched.

'New-found. . .five years on,' Penny said quietly.

Clive put down his glass. 'And do you know why I couldn't phone you when I first got out to Africa?'

Her heart began to thump madly and she leaned forward over the starched white tablecloth, anxious to catch every detail of what she hoped wasn't going to be a flimsy excuse.

'Are you ready to order?' the waiter hovering behind Clive's chair asked.

Penny had never chosen her food so quickly. Taking no advice from either Clive or the waiter, she ordered the first starter that caught her eye on the menu, which happened to be pitta bread and a plate of *tahina*, sesame spread spiced with oil, garlic and lemon. For her main course she ordered *shakshooka*, described in English on the menu as a mixture of chopped meat and tomato sauce with an egg tossed on top.

Clive leaned across to say that she had chosen well because *shakshooka* was like a delicious Spanish omelette with meat.

'Good,' Penny said impatiently, wishing Clive would make his order quickly so that they could return to their conversation.

'So why couldn't you contact me from Africa?' she began again as soon as the waiter had gone back to the kitchen.

He drew in his breath. 'I was involved in a car crash.'

'Oh. . . I'm sorry.' The words sounded trite and inadequate, but Clive seemed very calm and unworried about the situation. 'Were you badly hurt?'

'I don't remember the first two weeks, but I'm told I drifted in and out of consciousness. They had to fly me from the Matalan bush over the border to the university hospital at Ibadan in Nigeria. I was in Intensive Care for about a month. I had a fractured pelvis, a fractured scaphoid on my right wrist and a Colles' fracture on my left arm, several broken ribs and respiratory problems, so I was on a ventilator. By the time I was able to phone you——'

'You actually phoned me?' Her voice rose incredulously.

'Oh, spare me the dramatics! As if you didn't know!' he snapped, his eyes flashing angrily.

'Clive, I swear, I——'

'Let me finish,' he cut in harshly. 'And then you

can give me your excuses. You can tell me why you abandoned me when I needed you.'

'Clive, you must believe me when——' she began, but Clive ignored her interruption.

'They brought me a phone into Intensive Care and Sister Jane held it to my ear so I could call you. She was listening in, but I didn't mind. I just wanted to speak to you. I was furious when Victor answered.'

'Victor answered?' she echoed in disbelief.

'How can you pretend to look so surprised?' Clive glared at her across the table. 'Your boyfriend took a great delight in telling me you were living together. Can you imagine how I felt? After all we'd meant to each other on that wonderful night, how could you go straight into the arms of another man?'

'We were *not* living together.' She lowered her voice, aware of the glances of an expensively dressed Egyptian couple on the next table. 'Victor is like a brother to me. I'm sure you must have jumped to the wrong conclusion.'

Suddenly the light began to dawn as her memory of five years before cleared. 'I remember now; Victor's landlady had refused to give him any more credit. He'd spent his rent money and didn't dare ask his father for any more. So, temporarily, I let him sleep on the sofa in my living-room until he'd finished his second-year medical exams.'

In her mind's eye she could see Victor sprawled on her sofa, surrounded by his medical textbooks, during those hot summer weeks. She'd longed to get rid of him and have the place to herself again, but the poor boy had had nowhere to go. She remembered how his nerves had been on edge because of the exams and he'd done nothing but complain about the noise of the builders putting in a new kitchen for Mrs Roberts, her upstairs neighbour. He'd threatened to go up and complain to Mrs Roberts and the builders, but Penny had persuaded him that her landlord would turn him out if he did.

'Yes, it's all coming back to me,' she said out loud. 'Victor certainly made himself at home in my flat, but we weren't living together in the way that you're implying. I was longing to have the place to myself again, but I hadn't the heart to turn him out. We'd had a good platonic relationship since we were kids.'

Clive leaned back in his chair. His eyes were alarmingly hostile as he watched her. 'Well, he certainly gave the impression you were more than just good friends. He explained that you were on duty. I asked him to tell you that I was in Ibadan Hospital, Nigeria, following a car crash. He replied that you'd told him our affair had been a dreadful mistake and you didn't want to renew contact in any circumstances.'

The waiter arrived with their starters. It was impossible to remonstrate until they were alone again. Penny had totally lost her appetite, but she made a pretence of eating a few mouthfuls of pitta and *tahina* before putting her fork down on the plate.

'You must believe me, Clive; I never said anything of the sort. I think you must have still been in a coma. . .you must have imagined it.'

Now it was Clive's turn to raise his voice. 'I did not imagine it. And it was obvious from what Victor said that you'd been discussing me.'

'I may have mentioned you briefly, but it was only after——'

'After what, Penny?'

She took a deep breath. Not now. . . She couldn't tell him about the miscarriage.

'It was only after about three months, when it was obvious you weren't going to contact me, that I told Victor all about you. I needed somebody to talk to and Victor has always been so kind.'

'He was utterly convincing about your relationship, Penny,' Clive countered icily. 'It sounded as if you regretted you'd ever met me. . .that you wanted to forget that night we spent together. . .that wonderful night.'

She heard the huskiness in his voice and raised her eyes to his. The tender expression was back again. 'But why didn't you write to me and give me your address?'

His eyes flickered and then he spoke with ominous calm. 'I did.'

'But you couldn't have! I waited day after day for a letter from you and. . .'

She broke off as the waiter came to collect the plates and replace the starters with their main course. This time she made no attempt to eat anything, simply staring across the table at Clive, waiting for him to wriggle out of the corner she'd placed him in.

He leaned towards her across the table, his accusatory eyes boring inside her. 'It makes me furious to think that you're pretending not to believe me. Now, just listen while I tell you what happened as precisely as I can remember it. . . Sister Jane took the phone from me and said I'd been talking long enough and that I was to rest. I told her I was worried about the phone call I'd just made. . .that I had to make sure of certain facts. I asked her to help me write a letter. Again she told me to rest, but she promised to come back when she was off duty. I think I fell asleep for a while. . . I was so exhausted.'

He picked up his fork and started toying absently with a piece of grilled chicken. 'But I remember it was that same evening that she came back. I must have slept for a few hours. It was dark outside and they'd lifted me on to a bed and strung me up in a pelvic sling. My ribs were hurting and Sister Jane gave me a shot of pethidine. . .but not until after we'd finished the letter.'

'How did you manage to write a letter with both arms out of action?'

She felt utterly cruel to be examining Clive in this cold-blooded way, but she had to be sure he was telling the truth. She couldn't believe that Victor — honest, reliable, salt-of-the-earth Victor — would have double-crossed her over the phone call. It simply wasn't in his nature to invent the story that they were living together and that she didn't want anything to do with Clive. One of them must be lying. . .or maybe Clive had been in such a bad semi-comatosed state that he'd simply dreamed all this.

ARE YOU A FAN OF MILLS & BOON MEDICAL ROMANCES?

IF YOU are a regular United Kingdom buyer of Mills & Boon Medical Romances you might like to tell us your opinion of the books we publish to help us in publishing the books *you* like.

Mills & Boon have a Reader Panel of Medical Romance readers. Each person on the panel receives a questionnaire every third month asking her for *her* opinion of the past twelve Medical Romances. All people who send in their replies have a chance of winning a FREE year's supply of Medical Romances.

If YOU would like to be considered for inclusion on the Panel please give us details about yourself below. We can't guarantee that everyone will be on the panel but first come will be first considered. All postage will be free. Younger readers are particularly welcome.

Year of birth .... Month ....

Age at completion of full-time education ....

Single ☐ Married ☐ Widowed ☐ Divorced ☐

If any children at home, their ages please ....

Your name (print please) ....

Address ....

....

.... Postcode ....

THANK YOU! PLEASE TEAR OUT AND POST NO STAMP NEEDED IN THE U.K.

DR0993/RD

12

Do not affix Postage Stamps if posted in Gt. Britain, Channel Islands or N. Ireland

BUSINESS REPLY SERVICE
Licence No. SF195

MILLS & BOON READER PANEL
P.O. BOX 152,
SHEFFIELD S11 8TE

Postage will be paid by Mills & Boon Limited

REWARD! Free Books! Free Gifts!

PLAY MILLS & BOON'S
LUCKY CARNIVAL WHEEL

SCRATCH HERE

8 19 27 32 15 6 2 24 13

FIND OUT IF YOU CAN GET FREE BOOKS AND A MYSTERY GIFT!

If offer card is missing, write to: Mills & Boon Reader Service, P.O. Box 236, Croydon, Surrey CR9 3RU

PLAY THE
LUCKY CARNIVAL WHEEL
and get as many as
SIX FREE GIFTS..

HOW TO PLAY:

1. With a coin, carefully scratch away the silver panel opposite. Then check your number against the numbers opposite to find out how many gifts you're eligible to receive.

2. You'll receive brand-new Mills & Boon Romances and possibly other gifts - ABSOLUTELY FREE! Return this card today and we'll promptly send you the free books and the gifts you've qualified for!

3. We're sure that, after your specially selected free books, you'll want more of these heartwarming Romances. So unless we hear otherwise, every month we will send you our 6 latest Romances for just £1.80 each * - the same price in the shops. Postage and Packing are free - we pay all the extras!
* Please note prices may be subject to VAT.

4. Your satisfaction is guaranteed! You may cancel or suspend your subscription at any time, simply by writing to us. The free books and gifts remain yours to keep.

NO COST! NO RISKS!
NO OBLIGATION TO BUY

FREE! THIS CUDDLY TEDDY BEAR!

You'll love this little teddy bear. He's soft and cuddly with an adorable expression that's sure to make you smile.

PLAY THE LUCKY "CARNIVAL WHEEL"

Scratch away the silver panel. Then look for your number below to see which gifts you're entitled to!

YES! Please send me all the free books and gifts to which I am entitled. I understand that I am under no obligation to purchase anything ever. If I choose to subscribe to the Mills & Boon Reader Service I will receive 6 brand new Romances for just £10.80 every month (subject to VAT). There is no charge for postage and packing. I may cancel or suspend my subscription at anytime simply by writing to you. The free books and gifts are mine to keep in anycase. I am over 18 years of age.

MS/MRS/MISS/MR _____

ADDRESS _____

_____

_____ POSTCODE _____

SIGNATURE _____

9A3R

41	WORTH 4 FREE BOOKS, A FREE CUDDLY TEDDY AND FREE MYSTERY GIFT.	
29	WORTH 4 FREE BOOKS AND A FREE CUDDLY TEDDY.	
17	WORTH 4 FREE BOOKS.	
5	WORTH 2 FREE BOOKS.	

mps MAILING PREFERENCE SERVICE

Offer expires 31st March 1994. The right is reserved to change the terms of this offer or refuse an application. Readers overseas and in Eire please send for details. Southern Africa write to Book Services International Ltd., P.O. Box 41654, Craighall, Transvaal 2024. You may be mailed with offers from other reputable companies as a result of this application. If you would prefer not to share in this opportunity please tick box. ☐

MORE GOOD NEWS FOR SUBSCRIBERS ONLY!

When you join the Mills & Boon Reader Service, you'll also get our free monthly Newsletter; featuring author news, horoscopes, competitions, special subscriber offers and much, much more!

Mills & Boon Reader Service
FREEPOST
P.O. Box 236
Croydon
Surrey
CR9 9EL

NO STAMP NEEDED

'Sister Jane was very kind. She took down my letter as I dictated it to her. Then she signed it and explained at the bottom of the page that I was unable to write. And the letter asked you to contact the hospital at Ibadan.'

Penny was totally confused. She didn't know what to believe as she leaned back in her chair and ran a hand through her long dark hair. The strands felt damp with nervous perspiration, but her hands were clammy and cold. 'Tell me about this Sister Jane.'

'She was specialling me at the time.'

'What was her surname?'

'Does it matter?' he snapped impatiently. 'She left soon afterwards to work in Hong Kong.'

'How convenient!' The words slipped out before Penny could stop them. The story was all too implausible — a car crash that silenced Clive for weeks, a phone call that never happened, a missing letter written by a sister with no surname who moved on.

Clive's eyes were glinting dangerously. 'So you don't believe me. Then give me one good reason why I should believe that Victor wasn't your live-in lover and that you hadn't told him you didn't want to see me again.'

A flicker of hope crossed her mind and then died as soon as it arrived. As she thought about the fact that Clive had known Victor's name, she remembered that day back at the Luxor hotel when she'd taken the phone call from Victor. Clive had been in the room when she'd said, 'Hello, Victor'. He'd even told her in a jocular way to give his regards to

Victor, as a parting shot when he'd left her room. So he would have easily remembered the name.

'I suppose it all boils down to the fact that neither of us trusts the other one,' she said quietly. 'It's not much of a basis for a relationship, is it?'

Clive threw his napkin down on the table and signalled to the waiter. 'Let's get out of here. We can't pretend to enjoy our meal when there's so much at stake.'

The moon was shining on the water as Clive put his arm around her waist and pulled her along the sandy path that led away from the bright lights of the restaurant to the edge of the sea. Reluctantly, she allowed herself to be swept along, knowing that perhaps this would be the last time they would try to sort things out between them. They'd reached stalemate; there seemed to be no way out. She'd wanted to go back to the Red Sea Hotel but Clive had insisted they take a walk before he drove away from Abdou's restaurant. The moon was teasing the gentle waves, glimmering gold in patches and crimson in others. It was a glorious night for lovers. Penny wished they could start afresh. . .hold a truce and pretend they'd only just met for the first time. She would be able to fall in love again with this tantalising man.

Clive stopped at the edge of the sea and pulled her towards him. She stood stock-still in the enclosure of his arms. She felt so safe. . .and so excited. It was almost as if their sparring in the restaurant had sharpened her appetite for the sensual pleasures they'd shared together.

He pulled her closer until she was pressed against the hard, muscular chest that was covered only by a thin silk shirt. She could imagine the suntanned skin of his chest covered with coarse black hair. It had aroused her the first time. It would drive her wild the second. . .if ever there were to be a second.

She opened her mouth to speak, but his demanding lips silenced her. His hands were caressing her body, smoothing the soft contours of her blouse and then her skirt. She leaned against him, revelling in the erotic current that was passing between them. She felt as if she were drownng in sensual sensations. But the brief moment passed. Clive had pulled away from her and was looking down with tender eyes.

'Why don't we pretend the past doesn't exist?' he murmured. 'Does it matter what happened five years ago?'

She shook her head as she tried so hard to blot out the memories of her disillusionment. This time it would be different. 'It doesn't matter at all, Clive,' she whispered hoarsely.

And at that precise moment she meant it. It was only later that the reality of the situation hit her. But for that night she wanted to belong again to Clive.

His kiss was tender, then more demanding, until they both clung to each other in passionate desperation. He picked her up in his arms and carried her over to a group of palm trees at the edge of the narrow beach. Gently he laid her down and covered her face with kisses. She responded with glorious abandon. All the pent-up longing of five years was released.

She opened her eyes to stare up at the moon. Clive's tantalising fingers were caressing her. She felt so alive, so vibrant, so uninhibited. This was where she belonged. . .but for how long?

A cloud was passing over the moon. Her head was trying to conquer her heart. Somewhere deep inside her the still small voice of reason was telling her to hold back. If she gave herself totally to Clive now he would treat her as he had done before. She would be yesterday's love and he would walk out of her life again.

'No, Clive!' She pushed against his strong chest. 'I don't want to make love. . .not here. . .not now. . .'

His eyes were troubled in the moonlight as he relaxed his embrace.

'Second thoughts?' he asked, his voice husky with passion.

'It's second time around that worries me,' she whispered.

'I thought we were going to pretend we were first-time lovers,' he rasped.

'I thought so too. . .but not yet. I need to be sure that I won't get hurt again.'

He pulled her close into his arms again. 'Would it make any difference if I told you I loved you, Penny?'

She felt a surge of happiness. 'I think it might.'

'Well, let's have a fresh start. Stop torturing yourself about the past. It can't have been all that bad for you. I was the one who had the car crash. I had to lie there week after week wondering why our love had meant nothing to you. You simply had to carry on as normal with your old life. No, hear me out,' he insisted as Penny tried to remonstrate. 'The only solution is to forget the past and start afresh. What do you say?'

Penny looked up at the leaves swaying in the palm trees and drew in her breath. 'I'll try,' she said quietly.

His kiss was as light as a butterfly's wing. And then he led her back along the path to his car. The touch of his fingers around her waist was sending shivers of excitement down her spine. But she wouldn't give in to the clamouring of her heart. Once she could be sure that Clive was telling the truth she would give in. But until then she would try to hold back.

CHAPTER EIGHT

DURING the night, as she tossed and turned, Penny had managed to convince herself that Clive was telling the truth. Why would he lie? She would contact Victor as soon as possible and find out what had actually been said in that far-off phone call. It must have been a total misunderstanding. It had to be. And, having convinced herself, she allowed herself to remember Clive's sensual, husky voice when he'd told her he loved her.

Well, he hadn't actually said the three little words on their own, but he'd asked her if it would make any difference if he told her he loved her, which was the same thing. . .wasn't it?

As she went on duty next morning she felt as if she were walking on cloud nine. Nothing and no one could upset her in the clinic. She was sure the romantic glow suffusing her whole body would be patently obvious to everyone, but she didn't care. When Clive walked in through the treatment-room door she felt her legs go weak and wobbly again. He strode across and gave her that secret, tender look she'd come to regard as her own before he turned to smile at the other members of the medical team.

'Good morning, ladies.'

Staff Nurse Aziza and Auxiliary Nurse Samia smiled back, their adoring eyes showing their affection for their well respected medical director. Neither of them had approved of the doctor Clive had dismissed and they were both hoping that Clive would stay on without appointing a successor. He'd explained that he was only there in a temporary capacity as he had to move around all the ICMWT clinics in a supervisory capacity.

'Sister, would you come into the consulting-room for a minute or two? I won't keep you long.'

'Of course.' Penny tried to put on a professional air as she followed Clive across the room, aware of the nurses' eyes upon her.

There were a couple of patients waiting on the seats outside the consulting-room. Clive nodded pleasantly. 'We'll be with you in a few minutes. Won't keep you long.'

He unlocked the door and held it open for Penny to go inside. She had only taken two steps into the room before he closed the door and swept her into his arms.

'My darling,' he whispered against her hair.

As she revelled in their long, lingering kiss she wondered how she could ever have doubted his sincerity. Simply being together last night had been so wonderful, so out of this world; her skin was still tingling with the memory of it.

She laughed as she moved in his arms. 'How am I ever going to concentrate on anything with you around me?'

He smiled down at her, stroking one of the long, dark strands of hair that had escaped her cap. 'We'll both have to make the effort. On duty nothing must change...but off duty will be heaven...just as it was last night.'

She sighed. 'OK, Doctor, are we on or off duty now?'

He dropped a light kiss on her cheek. 'Definitely on duty, so let's get a move on. Bring in the first patient, please, Sister Byrne...but look in that mirror and straighten your cap first.'

She smiled at her reflection. Over her shoulder Clive was making funny faces at her. Oh, wasn't it wonderful to be in love again?

Her features composed, she brought in the first patient and the morning surgery began. More patients arrived to fill up the waiting-area. There were several upset tummies that had to be checked out in case there were serious problems. Samples had to be taken for pathology, and it all took time.

The clinic drew its patients not only from the Red Sea Hotel but also from several other hotels in the area. And there were also some of the Egyptians living near by who liked to avail themselves of the medical facilities at the clinic. No one was ever turned away.

The patients who'd over-indulged in sunbathing and burnt themselves were gently chided after their skin had been treated, in the hope that there wouldn't be a repetition of the problem.

'How can people be so foolish?' Penny said to Clive as they walked along the corridor to check on their in-patients at the end of the morning surgery. They had actually had to admit a young woman whose skin was in a dreadful state from too much solar exposure.

'It's usually the ones who come out for one week only and feel they must spend every minute in the sun. But they don't realise that a safe tan has to be acquired gradually. Talking of which, I thought we'd go out to one of the islands this afternoon.'

They paused outside Mona's room and Clive looked down at Penny, a tender smile playing on his lips. 'How does the idea suit you?'

She smiled. 'Sounds wonderful.' Her toes inside her sensible duty shoes seemed to curl up. The thought of a hot afternoon with Clive, swimming in the sea, sunbathing on the sand, and afterwards. . .

He was pushing open the patient's door and she followed inside.

Mona's baby was sucking at her breast, making gentle infantile grunts of satisfaction.

'How are you feeling, Mona?' Clive asked, placing his fingers on the pulse at her wrist.

The patient smiled. 'I'm fine. My tummy's a bit stiff and sore, but otherwise I feel great. I'd like to go home as soon as I can. My husband's staying with his mother, but it's a bit crowded there and he'd like to go back to our own little house.'

'But can't he look after himself?' Penny asked mischievously, knowing full well that Egyptian men were totally pampered first by their mothers and then by their wives.

Mona looked shocked at the suggestion. 'Of course he can't, Sister. He needs me for everything.'

'Well, he'll have to wait for a few days, Mona,'

Clive put in gently. 'I'm not going to allow you home until you're stronger. It's no good undoing all the good work we've put in so far.'

He bent down and placed his fingers over the anterior fontanelle on the baby's dark head, feeling for the full, bounding, healthy pulse. 'Have you chosen a name yet?'

Mona smiled proudly. 'My son will be called Mohammed after my father.'

'And after your brother as well,' Penny said.

'And my brother,' Mona echoed.

Penny asked if it wouldn't be confusing to have three Mohammeds in the family and Mona looked surprised at the suggestion.

'No, it won't be confusing, Sister. Mohammed is a very popular name in Egypt. . .and a very proud name too.'

Mona looked down adoringly at her new-born son and the expression in the maternal eyes gave Penny another feeling of satisfaction at the part she and Clive had played in this successful birth.

They skipped lunch and took a picnic in a wicker basket from the hotel kitchens. After driving a couple of miles along the side of the Red Sea they came to a small harbour where several varieties of boats were moored.

As soon as they stepped out of the car into the sweltering midday heat they were inundated with requests from the sailors who wanted them to hire a boat.

'How about a submarine cruise?' Clive asked

Penny, trying to ignore the pressure that was being put upon them by the eager boat crews.

'A submarine?' Penny echoed doubtfully. 'I thought we were going to go swimming.'

'We can have our swim and picnic later.' He shaded his eyes and pointed across the harbour. 'The boat over there that's just about to leave will take us out to the submarine. I'm told we only stay down for about an hour and then——'

'An hour!'

Clive shrugged. 'Oh, well, if you don't like the idea. The boat's going now, anyway.'

'Oh, let's go!' Penny said impulsively. She loved new experiences, but was slightly overawed by the possibility of feeling claustrophobic.

But once on board the transfer boat her confidence returned. Most of the other people looked older and more relaxed than she was. If they could contemplate submerging themselves in the depths of the Red Sea, then so could she.

Sitting beside Clive at the back of the boat, she could feel the wind rustling through her hair. It was good to get out on to the sea after the hot, dry atmosphere inland. Over on one side of the boat she could see the tall hills rising up like sentries guarding the vast wastes of the desert that separated them from the verdant valley of the Nile, and on the other side were the tiny islands, sprinkled liberally in coral clusters over the middle of the Red Sea.

They were approaching a wide wooden platform to which a small, bright yellow submarine was attached. As they clambered on to the platform

Penny could see that the submarine was a huge attraction for the tourists, but she was relieved to find that, even though it was small, it appeared authentic in every detail. She remarked on this to Clive as they waited to board the submarine.

He smiled. 'How would you know it was authentic? Are you an expert on submarines?'

She laughed. 'Well, it looks like all the submarines I've ever seen in war films. Thank goodness we're not in a state of war now! Wouldn't it be awful if when we got down there we were in danger of being torpedoed! I don't mind telling you, I'm a bit scared simply of submerging.'

He put an arm around her waist. 'You'll be OK. The submarine has to undergo frequent rigorous testing and the crew are highly skilled. They wouldn't dare put the lives of all these tourists at risk. Think of the bad publicity!'

So that was what Penny thought about as she waited patiently for her turn to descend. The submarine had to be one hundred per cent safe. And she had to admit that the sailors who manned it looked extremely competent in their smart, gold-braided uniforms.

Nevertheless there were butterflies in her stomach as she climbed through the narrow, round hatch and down the iron-runged ladder into the bowels of the machine. There was room for forty-six passengers and two crew. The passengers each had their own seat facing the large easy-vision portholes, and individual monitoring screens showed what was happening above and below the water.

Clive sat down beside her and put a hand on her shoulder. 'Are you still OK?'

She smiled. 'Fine.'

As she glanced at the elderly white-haired man seated on the other side of her, she thought that, if he was happy to make the journey, then she must try to look as if she was enjoying it.

The hatch was closed with a loud clang and the submarine began to submerge. Penny watched her monitoring screen and saw that they'd left the landing-platform behind. She looked out of her porthole and watched the multi-coloured fish swimming past. A diver plunged down through the middle of the shoal, scattering some kind of food which the fish attacked with great relish. Then the diver broke an egg and the fish became frenzied with excitement as they nuzzled each other out of the way in an effort to appease their appetites. Penny had to remind herself that she was at the bottom of the sea and not in some aquatic theatre on dry land watching a spectacular show.

The minutes passed and she forgot her initial misgivings as she watched the fascinating scene. She put a hand to her neck to loosen her collar, realising it was getting hotter inside the cabin. Turning her head, she saw that because the submarine was now stationary the two gold-braided sailors were able to take it easy in the front section, which resembled the cockpit of an aircraft with its complicated-looking instrument panel.

Suddenly, she became aware that the elderly man beside her was having problems. His plump, grey-haired, motherly wife was leaning across him, holding his hand and speaking soothingly to him.

'It won't be long now, Harry. You'll be OK. Just take deep breaths.'

But Penny could see at a glance that the man was becoming dangerously cyanosed and was in obvious pain. This was no ordinary attack of nerves. She turned to Clive and alerted him in a quiet voice, so as not to alarm the other passengers.

Clive moved quickly to kneel beside the man, who was by this time clutching his chest, and made a brief examination and preliminary diagnosis.

'I think it's a cardiac arrest,' Clive whispered into Penny's ear. 'Go into the forward section and ask the captain to resurface at once. Explain the situation and tell him there's no time to lose. This man is dangerously ill.'

Even as Clive spoke, the man keeled over and lost consciousness. Penny moved swiftly to the front of the vessel and alerted the crew, who were immediately sympathetic to the emergency situation.

'Give him mouth-to-mouth while I work on his chest,' Clive said in an urgent voice as soon as she returned.

It was no longer possible nor desirable to keep the rest of the passengers in the dark about the situation. The captain made a brief announcement over the loudspeaker, asking for full co-operation from everyone. A kindly middle-aged couple had taken charge of the distraught wife and were trying to reassure and comfort her.

'He's a doctor and I think she's a nurse,' the

couple were saying to the worried wife, and this seemed to give her hope.

Clive had succeeded in lying their patient flat across four seats. He was placing the heel of both hands on top of one another over the lower part of the sternum, depressing it firmly and then releasing it at a rate of about twelve times a minute.

Penny bent her head, took a deep breath, and began the mouth-to-mouth resuscitation. She had revived patients before like this, but never in such cramped conditions. Pinching her patient's nostrils with her fingers, she sealed her lips around his mouth and blew into his lungs. There was no response. She tried again...and again...and then, very slowly, in response to their combined efforts the patient's chest rose and he began to breathe again.

Clive sat back on his heels. 'He's going to make it!'

An audible sigh of relief went round the passengers. Penny pulled her hair out of her eyes. it had been falling over her face all the time she was attempting the resuscitation, but she hadn't dared break off. Clive put a hand on her arm.

'Thanks, Penny,' he whispered, his eyes mirroring her relief.

'What now?' she asked quietly, cradling the patient's head in her arms as she thought that he was in no way out of danger. The immediate crisis had been dealt with, but the journey back to full medical facilities would be crucial.

'I'll get a helicopter,' Clive said. 'You stay here while I speak to the captain.'

The helpful couple were coping with the patient's wife, who was becoming calmer now that she could see that Penny and Clive were firmly in control of the situation. The submarine had reached the surface and was tied up once again to the landing-platform. As the passengers filed off there wasn't one of them who protested at having had a shorter trip than usual. They were all sympathetic to the life-threatening emergency.

'What's your husband's name?' Penny gently asked the patient's wife.

'Harry Smith, and I'm Vera. He's seventy-two next birthday. I told him he wasn't up to larking about like a two-year-old but would he listen?'

'Has he ever had any problems with his heart, Mrs Smith?' Clive, who had instructed the captain to radio for a rescue helicopter, now reappeared and sat down beside the patient's wife.

'Not that I know of,' Vera Smith replied thoughtfully. 'But he's had a few twinges lately. But we put it down to indigestion...you know how you do,' she finished in an apologetic tone.

Penny looked at Clive and knew they were both thinking the same thing. Nobody ever took these 'twinges' seriously until it was too late and they were floored by a full-scale cardiac arrest.

'So your husband has never had an ECG...an electrocardiogram to check out his heart?' Clive asked.

Mrs Smith shook her head. 'Oh, no, nothing like that. You see, he's always been so fit, has Harry.

There's been no need. Well, he's not the one to go running to the doctor, isn't Harry.'

They could hear the welcome sound of the helicopter circling overhead.

'That was quick!' Penny said. 'I suppose they have a helicopter always at the ready because of the number of diving activities in the Red Sea.'

Clive nodded. 'I've requested a stretcher and an oxygen mask.'

Penny glanced down at her patient. He was still cyanosed, although breathing more regularly now. The sooner they got an oxygen mask over his face the better.

There was a loud noise above them as the helicopter landed on the wooden platform. Two Egyptian medical orderlies climbed swiftly down the ladder, carrying a stretcher between them.

Clive took charge of the delicate hoisting operation that was necessary to bring their patient up from the cabin. When they reached the platform Penny noticed that all the passengers had been taken away by the transfer boat.

Clive, still supervising the carrying of the stretcher, put a hand under Vera Smith's arm and helped her board the helicopter. Penny followed and took her place beside the patient. One of the crew closed the helicopter door and in seconds they were airborne.

It was thrilling to be doing an almost vertical takeoff. What a day! First Penny had been taken to the depths of the sea and now she was winging her way over it, the wind created by the helicopter scattering the low-flying seagulls. One enormous bird was so surprised that it dropped the fish it had just plucked from the water. Penny saw a dart of silver below the sea and she felt sure that the fish had escaped unharmed beneath the white-capped waves.

She looked back at her patient, reaching for the pulse at his wrist. It was much steadier and his face enclosed by the oxygen mask was a better colour.

She let out an audible sigh of relief. Clive, sitting beside her, squeezed her hand.

'Sorry about the picnic,' he whispered.

She smiled. 'I'd forgotten all about it. I suppose we'll have to pick up the car from the harbour when we've settled our patient.'

'If all goes well with him I'll get someone to drive us out there this evening. The food will still be OK because I put the perishables in the cold container. We could have a midnight picnic out on one of the islands. . .but we'd better see how things go,' he whispered. 'We could well be on duty all night.'

Penny turned to look at the patient's wife. Mrs Smith appeared calm and in control of herself again. She was looking out of the window of the helicopter and now seemed to be taking her husband's illness in her stride.

Two hours later Clive and Penny had the situation fully under control. Harry Smith was settled in one of their private rooms, having undergone extensive tests. Penny had fixed up an oxygen tent and ensured that a nurse was specialling their patient at all times. Vera Smith had also insisted on staying in the room with her husband and was now asleep in an armchair, her plump ankles fixed on a low bamboo stool.

Penny had tried to persuade Mrs Smith to sleep in one of the other rooms, but the elderly lady had been worried about the cost of all the expensive treatment. No matter that Clive had explained that ICMWT was a non-profit-making organisation financed by an international consortium of industrialists and businessmen whose aim was to ensure that only those patients who could afford the fees had to pay anything, and also that the Smiths were covered by travel insurance. The dear lady was still convinced that someone would present her with a hefty bill.

Penny smiled as she remembered hearing Mrs Smith's voice rambling on in her sleep in the armchair a few moments ago.

'Never owed a penny in my life...not going to start now...'

Penny pulled off her uniform and lay down on the narrow bed in her hotel room. Her surroundings weren't as luxurious as those at the Nile Hotel, but it was clean, comfortable and charming with its matching flowered cotton bedspread and curtains. And she was only yards from the sea so that she could hear the sound of the waves on the shore. Glancing at the bedside clock, she saw it was already ten o'clock. What a day! She felt whacked but knew that what she needed was a relaxing evening rather than an early night. Her thoughts turned to Clive's mad idea of a midnight picnic.

Was it still on? Her pulses began to race at the prospect of a midnight swim in the warm Red Sea with Clive. Surely this was playing with fire. . . She wouldn't be able to hold out against him. But did she want to hold out. . .was there any need for it? Surely she was convinced that he'd made that phone call to her. . .that he'd sent her a letter. . .wasn't she?

Oh, if only she could be sure!

Impulsively, she picked up the bedside phone. It was now or never. With the two-hour time difference it would only be eight o'clock in England. With any luck Victor would still be somewhere around his father's surgery. There were always patients who arrived well into the evening, and old Dr Robinson had earned the reputation of never turning anyone away even if he was in the middle of his supper.

She dialled Reception and gave them the number, requesting a person-to-person call to Dr Victor Robinson. She didn't want to have to speak to Victor's father. However kindly the old man was, he would naturally be curious about her reason for making an expensive international call. And the news would no doubt filter back to her mother. Mrs Byrne thought the world of their family doctor and was always singing his praises. She'd often told Penny how old Dr Robinson had trudged through the snow twenty-five years ago to deliver her when all the motorised transport had ground to a halt. And he'd continued to come out on house calls long after many doctors had started plugging themselves into a deputising switchboard that would find a locum for them during the night.

The hotel receptionist's voice cut through her nostalgic thoughts. 'I will call you, Sister. It will be several minutes before I can put you through.'

'Thank you. I'll wait by the phone.' She lay back on the bed, staring up at the whirring fan in the centre of the ceiling. She'd waited so long for the mystery to be solved. Another few minutes wouldn't make much difference.

It was six minutes before the phone rang, and they were the longest minutes she'd ever experienced.

'Penny, how wonderful to hear from you! Nothing wrong, I hope?'

'No, everything's fine, Victor.'

They indulged in another minute of banal small talk before Penny took the plunge.

'I wonder if you can cast your mind back to five years ago, Victor. Do you remember getting a phone call from Clive Hamilton?'

Silence for a few seconds and then, 'No; why would Clive Hamilton want to phone me? Five years ago I was only a poor medical student and the illustrious Dr Hamilton wouldn't have wasted a phone call on the likes of me.'

'Well. . .he seems to think he spoke to you. He was actually ringing me at my flat. He said you answered. . .told him you were living with me. . . I mean living there as——'

She broke off, hearing the peals of laughter drifting over the miles. 'The man must be mad. You know what he's trying to do, don't you?'

'No, but I'm sure you'll tell me.'

'He's trying to get you back after he dumped you five years ago. He's hoping you'll forget what a swine he was, going off and leaving you pregnant like that——'

'Victor, please!' Oh, God, anyone could be listening in to their call. 'I only wanted to know if you'd taken a call from him, that was all. He says he phoned me and you say he didn't. I don't know who to believe.'

There was an ominous silence. For an instant Penny thought Victor had put the phone down.

'Victor? Are you still there?'

'I'm here, but I'm hurt at the suggestion that I might lie to you. Who was it who picked up the pieces when you were almost suicidal?'

'Look, I'm truly grateful, Victor. But you must see it from my point of view. I have to get at the truth because...because, well, the fact of the matter is that I think I still love him.' She took a deep breath. 'I mean I *know* I still love him. Nothing can change my feelings.'

Again the unnerving silence. This time she waited for Victor to express his predictably damning opinion of the situation.

'Penny, you know of course that your Clive Hamilton is married?'

Now it was Penny's turn to be speechless. She could hear Victor calling her name, but the room seemed to be spinning round. Of course, that would account for Clive's reluctance to give her full details of the last five years.

At length, she found her voice. 'No, I didn't know. Are you absolutely sure?'

'Of course I'm sure. There's a new registrar down at the hospital. He was out in West Africa five years ago. We were talking one evening at a dinner party and I asked him if he'd ever come across Clive Hamilton. He told me that they'd met on a couple of social occasions organised by their wives.'

'And you're sure it was Clive's he was talking about?'

'Oh, yes, he said Clive's wife was perfectly charming.'

Someone was knocking on the door.

'Look, Victor, I'll have to go. . .but thank you for your information.'

'Penny, don't do anything stupid,' Victor said.

'I won't,' she replied in a grim voice.

The knocking on the door had turned into a persistent hammering. She flung open the door.

'Good God, Penny. I've been trying to get through on the phone and now when I actually arrive it's like getting into Fort Knox.'

He began to walk into the room, but she held both hands in front of her.

'Please don't come any further, Clive. I want to be alone. I'm tired. Please, just go away and let me think.'

His face took on a look of tender consternation. 'Darling, what's happened? Have you had some bad news?'

'Bad news, good news, what's the difference?' Her voice rose to a barely controlled shriek, but she held her ground, her eyes fixed on his face with a menacing glare.

'I've come to take you out... Everything's arranged. I've got a taxi waiting to take us down to the harbour. You need a break.'

'I'm all right. Just go away,' she said quietly, afraid that the tears would flow before she could close the door.

'But we've got to spend this evening together! I've had a calling asking me to go back to Luxor tomorrow. Ahmed Fakry is having problems he can't sort out. We've agreed to change places for a few weeks. Darling, this will be our last chance to be alone together. Tell me your troubles and we can share them.'

He was reaching out to take her in his arms, but she moved away.

'No, Clive. Not now. I have to think... You can't help me. Just leave me alone.'

'You're so difficult!'

She heard his deep sigh of impatience before he brushed his lips across her cheek. She closed her eyes as she heard the sound of his footsteps walking off down the corridor. She imagined she could see the moon shining on the Red Sea, feel the sand running through her toes as she curled up against Clive on the shore of a deserted island. She opened her mouth to call him back, to tell him that whatever lies he'd told her she would forgive him. Because her deep-down gut reaction was to believe him... but all the facts seemed to prove otherwise.

CHAPTER NINE

BY THE middle of November, Penny had got used to working with Dr Ahmed Fakry again. It seemed ages since she'd seen Clive, but it was actually only a matter of a few weeks. She'd thrown herself wholeheartedly into doing a good job at the clinic on the Red Sea, but the uncertainty of her relationship with Clive hadn't helped. There were some days when she found it a real effort to put on a smile when she went into the consulting-room at the start of morning surgery.

One morning Dr Fakry commented on this, causing her some embarrassment.

'Is anything wrong, Penny? You wouldn't by any chance be wishing I'd go back to Luxor so that Clive would have to return here, would you?'

Carefully she put down the sterile kidney dish on the examination trolley. She'd been on the point of calling in the first patient. Instead she turned to face Ahmed. Over the weeks she'd worked with the young Egyptian doctor she'd come to respect his skill and judgement in medical matters. So far she thought she'd kept him in the dark about her relationship with Clive. But she knew that tongues had been wagging. Rumours had been flying around the medical grape-vines both at Luxor and on the Red Sea and it would be pointless to make a denial.

'I think it's better if you stay here, Ahmed,' she said slowly. 'After all, there's no future in having a relationship with a married man.'

Ahmed's eyes were troubled. 'Clive isn't married . . . or at least if he is he keeps his wife well hidden. I've known him two years and there's been no mention of a Mrs Hamilton. I'm sure he would have brought her with him. After all, his job entails so much travelling he wouldn't want to have a lengthy separation.'

Penny's heart began to thud. She walked over to the window and looked out over the gardens that led down to the Red Sea. There was still an abundance of multi-coloured flowers giving the appearance of summer. But the Egyptian winter was advancing quickly. Overhead, the sun shone warmly during the day, but the evenings were cool and the nights positively cold. The cold nights reminded her of home and the fact that in a month she would be going back to England; then the brief renewal of her relationship with Clive would be over. She'd come to terms with this during the last week, when she'd convinced herself that she must avoid him at all costs. But the awful thing was that when she was given the slightest glimmer of hope — like just now when Ahmed contradicted the idea that Clive might be married — she felt herself swimming back on to a rising tide of interest in the wretched man!

'Forgive me for interfering, Penny, but I felt I had to know what was going on between the two of you before. . .' Dr Fakry stopped in mid-sentence, as if searching for the right words.

'Before what?'

Now it was the courteous Egyptian who looked embarrassed. 'Well, last week Clive phoned up to ask me if you could go back to Luxor to work with him over there. He asked me to make the necessary staffing arrangements in the clinic here. . .and I've been somewhat slow about doing so. In fact I've taken much longer than was absolutely necessary. I know of a nursing sister who would be only too happy to step into your shoes tomorrow. . .if that's what you would like.'

Penny walked back across the room and sat down in the chair across the desk from Ahmed.

'You are very kind to be concerned, Ahmed, but you see I needed to distance myself from Clive. . . for various reasons. When he rang me from Luxor a couple of times recently, I was deliberately cool and professional. I made it clear that whatever there had been between us was over.'

'I think you're being hard on both of you,' Dr Fakry said in a careful voice. 'I could see the spark that flared between you even on that first evening in Luxor. Whatever has happened to put out the flame should be rekindled. If it dies again. . .then so be it. But I don't think you can turn your back on Clive. I believe he too is suffering from this enforced separation. I'm sure he would have been over to see you if you hadn't pushed him away.'

The doctor stood up and came round the desk to put his hand on her shoulder. 'I you really don't want to see Clive again you'd better tell him, because I can't hold off this staff change much longer without Clive becoming suspicious. Leave the decision to the end of surgery.' He glanced up at the clock and became suddenly brisk and efficient. 'Would you bring in the first patient?'

Penny tried to put the problem to the back of her mind, but it kept bubbling up into her consciousness throughout the morning as she cared for her patients. When the last out-patient had left the consulting-room she went through into the in-patient section to check on Harry Smith, their cardiac patient.

She was pleased to find him sitting in a chair beside the bed, looking much fitter. Since his cardiac arrest when they were in the submarine on the Red Sea, Harry had been on bed-rest for most of the time, with emergency oxygen close at hand. But at last he was able to get up for part of the day and take a few cautious steps around the room. His wife, Vera, had settled back into their hotel room, having discovered that her tour company was prepared to pay the extra expense incurred due to Harry's illness.

Penny folded up her stethoscope after listening to Harry's chest.

'We'll soon be setting you free, Harry,' she told her patient.

'That's good news, Sister. Vera'll be pleased. She's dying to get back home and start on her Christmas shopping. She usually has everything finished before the end of November. But before we go, I would like to say goodbye to that other doctor . . .the English one you were with on the day I collapsed. I wouldn't have been here without him. The pair of you saved my life. What a team! To be honest, I thought you were sweet on each other.'

He was giving her a sideways glance, but she managed to stave off the blushes.

'You're fishing now, aren't you, Harry? Well, for the record, we're just good friends, nothing more.'

'Well, that's a pity. Anyway, could you get him to come in and see me before I'm discharged?'

'I'm afraid he's over at Luxor. If he comes back I'll certainly ask him to see you.'

She went back to the treatment-room to see if the nurses had finished clearing up. Young Mohammed was lounging by the door, a broom in one hand and a duster in the other.

'I didn't know you worked for us on Mondays, Mohammed. Shouldn't you be in school?' she asked.

'We've got a day off today because some bigwig politician is holding a meeting in the school. So I came in instead of Friday. There's always so much homework at the weekend. Since I told the teachers I intend to be a doctor they pile on the work, especially in science.'

Penny smiled. 'I'm glad you're taking your studies seriously. How's your sister Mona and the baby?'

Mohammed gave a broad, happy smile that brightened up the whole of his dark face. 'She's fine. Tell me, Sister, when's Dr Hamilton coming here again?'

She took a deep breath. 'I really couldn't say.'

'Sister. . .your decision, please!' Ahmed Fakry was striding across the room. 'Dr Hamilton is on the phone. Are you going to Luxor or staying here?'

She was aware that all eyes were on her. It was uncharacteristic of Ahmed to put her on the spot like this. He was obviously trying to force her hand.

'I'll speak to Dr Hamilton myself,' she said quietly as she went through into the deserted consulting-room and picked up the phone.

She took a deep breath. 'Hello, Clive.'

'I don't believe it! I was beginning to think you'd lost your voice, the number of times you've been unavailable. Are you alone. . .? Can you talk?'

'Better not,' she said hurriedly. 'I'll come over to Luxor and we can talk in private.'

'I think we should. I'm glad you're coming over. Better still, hold off for a couple of days and I'll join you over there. There are a couple of matters to attend to in Hurghada. Then we could spend more time swimming before going back to Luxor together.'

'Clive!'

'Yes?' Oh, God! The world and his wife were probably listening in! 'We'll have the talk before our swim.'

'Whenever you like,' he replied breezily and hung up.

For two days Penny's emotions swung wildly. One minute she wanted to ignore all her misgivings and go straight into a wild romance with Clive. The next she wanted to play safe, to interrogate him on every aspect of his life and drag all the skeletons out of the closet.

But when he walked in through the door of the

dining-room, looking hot and exhausted from his drive across the desert, she forgot everything except a passionate desire to be near him again.

He sat down opposite her at the table; she had Nurse Samia seated on one side of her and Staff Nurse Aziza on the other. It was impossible to talk about anything other than medical matters. Only once did their eyes meet and Penny deliberately looked away. She felt as if the whole of the dining-room was watching their reactions to each other.

They had reached the fruit and cheese stage. She pushed away her plate, finding it difficult to swallow. Her mouth seemed impossibly dry. She took a sip of bottled water before attempting to speak to Clive.

'Harry Smith was asking about you, Dr Hamilton,' she said, carefully raising her eyes to look across the table. 'He's going to be discharged at the end of next week.'

Clive smiled. Penny hadn't seen that smile for far too long, and her heart seemed to turn over. It was like the sun coming out at the end of a long dark winter.

'Perhaps we could go and see Mr Smith together, Sister. I'd like you to fill me in on the details of his treatment since I was here last.'

Clive was standing up, pushing back his chair, nodding to acquaintances across the dining-room. The room seemed to go unusually quiet. All eyes were definitely on Penny as she walked towards the door, Clive a few paces behind. They were in the corridor before he touched her. His hand on her arm sent shivers of excitement running through her as he spoke.

'Why the icy welcome? Aren't you pleased to see me? I stayed away as long as I could to give you time to get over what's troubling you. It seemed like a private matter, but I'm sure I could have helped if you hadn't chosen to be so tough and independent. Was there a problem at home? I remember the night I had to leave. You'd just taken a long phone call and——'

'Oh, Clive, not here!'

'Well, after we've seen Harry Smith I insist——'

'Yes, yes, I'll tell you then. We'll go somewhere where we can be alone.'

He put a hand under her arm as they went into their patient's room. 'Well, that sounds promising.'

'Dr Hamilton!' Harry Smith's wrinkled face lit up with a smile. 'Good to see you again.'

'And good to see you looking so well.' Clive picked up the charts and scanned them before sitting down beside his patient for a leisurely chat.

It was another hour before they were able to escape from the clinic together. Ahmed Fakry had assured Clive that there were no staffing problems, and he'd waved them off at the door of the hotel.

'It's almost as if Ahmed wants to get rid of us,' Clive said as he turned the Land Rover into the coastal road.

'I think he's anxious we should sort out our differences,' Penny said carefully.

'Well, I've got nothing to sort out, so fire away. What's your problem, Penny?'

She looked out across the blue sea towards the distant islands. It was pity to spoil such a beautiful day with unharmonious thoughts, but it was something she had to do. . .something she should have done when she'd first heard the awful news from Victor. She shouldn't have let the problem stew in her mind. She knew she'd lacked the courage to take the bull by the horns and learn the truth.

She took a deep breath as she looked sideways at Clive. His white open-necked polo shirt emphasised the deep tan of his skin. He looked so handsome. . . and so unapproachable. He would be furious when she told him she knew his secret.

'Clive. . .are you married?' She swallowed hard; her voice had cracked as soon as she'd pronounced his name.

His expression darkened with displeasure, but he kept his eyes on the sandy road ahead. 'Why do you ask?'

Oh, God, he hadn't denied it! Then it must be true. 'Because Victor told me on the phone that——'

'Ah, Victor. . .the wonderful knight in shining armour. What stories is he weaving about me now?'

'He told me you were married. He'd met someone who knew you in West Africa. . .someone who said that your wife was charming.'

Several seconds elapsed before Clive gave his reply in a hoarse whisper. 'And so she was.'

'Was?'

'Look, we'd better leave this conversation until

later. It's difficult enough negotiating this damn road without your interrogation.'

She bit her lip, unwilling to point out it was he who'd started the questioning.

He drove on in stony silence and Penny stared out of the window, wondering what kind of a hornets' nest she'd stirred up. There was a newly painted blue and white cabin cruiser waiting for them down by the harbour. It appeared that Clive had telephoned ahead to make the reservation. A crew of three Egyptian sailors was standing by, ready to help them on board.

The boat took off at speed across the water, heading for one of the semi-tropical islands. Neither of them broke their silence until they reached the sandy shore. The crew slung an iron ladder over the side and they climbed down.

'We don't want to be disturbed,' Clive told the captain after they had settled themselves on the deserted beach surrounded by towels, swimming gear, snorkels and picnic basket. 'You can leave us here for two hours.'

Penny watched as the crew returned to the boat moored some distance away. She looked around her. It was the nearest she'd ever been to a true Robinson Crusoe island. She felt like a castaway. Leaning back on the sand, she pulled a large beach towel around her shoulders and eased herself into her bikini. From the sound of it, Clive was changing too, but she didn't give him a sideways glance until she was sure he was in his swimming trunks.

What a physique! she thought as she allowed her

eyes to wander over the tanned body stretched out beside her. And then she caught sight of a long scar leading from the centre of his chest to the side. She put out her fingers and touched it as gently as she would if he'd been a patient.

'What's this, Clive?'

'Oh, that was where a couple of ribs came through . . .in the car crash I told you about. . .remember?'

'Yes. . .yes, I remember. Oh, Clive. . .' So the mythical car crash was a reality after all. Then what else was true? The wife?

He raised himself up on his elbows and stared down at her with a quizzical look. 'Do you know, I honestly think you didn't believe me. You're looking so astonished. Did you think I'd made the car crash up. . .did you?'

'I didn't know what to believe.'

'Well, believe this,' he told her in a grim voice. 'Everything I've told you is the truth. Two days after our wonderful night together in London I was driving through the West African bush in Matala, a small, undeveloped country to the east of Nigeria. It was raining. . .and when I say raining I don't mean the downpours we sometimes get in England. This was like standing under the shower for several hours. My African driver was very experienced, but even he was having difficulty negotiating the potholes in the red laterite road. . .'

Clive drew in his breath and pulled a hand over his eyes. Penny could see that the memory was deeply disturbing.

'Look, Clive, if you'd rather not talk about it. . .'

'You asked for the truth and you're going to get it,' he replied in a grim voice, turning away from her and lying back on the sand, one hand shielding his eyes from the sun's rays.

Penny lay back and closed her eyes as the story unfolded.

'I told my driver I thought we should stop until the storm had abated, but he said it could go on for hours and it would be unwise to stop in that part of the bush. He assured me that he'd driven through bad storms before. And it was at that point that it happened.'

Penny remained still and silent, scarcely daring to breathe as Clive continued in a subdued, husky voice.

'We rounded a bend in the muddy track and drove straight over the edge of a huge pothole. There had been a landslide, probably only minutes before. One minute we were driving along and the next we were hurtling down into a muddy crater. My seatbelt saved me, but my driver, who thought seatbelts were a useless contraption, was killed.'

'Clive, I'm so sorry.' She raised herself to look down at him, but his eyes were still covered by his hand. 'What happened?'

He took a deep breath. 'A rescue team found us two days later. I was conscious for some of those two days, but mercifully I kept sinking back into oblivion, so it wasn't too bad.'

He took his hand from his eyes and Penny was relieved to see that they were dry. She put out her hand and touched his forehead. He reached for her fingers and gently placed them against his lips.

The soft touch of his lips against her hand sent shivers of desire running through her. She snuggled against him and he held her in the crook of his arm, gently stroking her hair with smooth, sensual movements that roused rather than soothed the emotional turmoil inside her.

'And the rest, as they say, is history,' Clive finished off in a casual tone. 'I told you about my injuries. . .both arms out of action because of a fractured right scaphoid and a left Colles' fracture, a fractured pelvis and these ribs.'

Penny traced her fingers over the deep scar on Clive's chest. 'They did a good job on you. Where did you say you were taken?'

'They flew me over the border to Ibadan in Nigeria. The university hospital there is one of the best.'

'And it was from there that you phoned me, wasn't it?'

Clive nodded. 'Yes, I'll never forget how absolutely gutted I was when I got Victor instead of you.'

She swallowed hard. It was all so plausible now . . .except why would Victor lie?

'You're sure you weren't so comatosed that you dreamed you were phoning? Perhaps you meant to phone. . .it was in your subconscious and——'

'I made that phone call.'

'And you sent me a letter. . .well, that could have got lost in the post.'

'That's a possibility. But I know Sister Jane posted

it. I remember checking a couple of years later and she told me——'

'But you said she went to Hong Kong.'

His eyes flickered momentarily. 'She did. And I followed her months later for my convalescence. We'd corresponded regularly while I was still in hospital. I was angry and upset that you'd forgotten me so quickly. I knew it had been a whirlwind affair, but I'd thought our love was something special. Jane knew I needed looking after when I left hospital, and she suggested I fly out to Hong Kong. She had an apartment up on the Peak near the hospital where she was working. I stayed longer than I meant to because she was so good to me and I started to feel strong again.'

'So how long did you stay with this Sister Jane?'

'A couple of months. And then I asked her to marry me. There was no blinding passion between us. . .just a mutual need for each other. She gave up her job and came back to Africa with me. I carried on working for ICMWT and she was the perfect hostess. I learned just before I married her that she was suffering from leukaemia. She was in recession. When she regressed, after six months of marriage, I begged her to go back to England to get the best possible treatment. She knew as well as I did that leukaemia isn't inevitably fatal nowadays. But she insisted on staying, said a wife should be by her husband's side. Very stubborn was Sister Jane.'

'Why do you call her Sister Jane?' Penny asked softly.

'Defence mechanism, I suppose. I like to put my

life into compartments. If I think of her as the nursing sister who cared for me after the crash I don't grieve for her as a wife. She died on our first wedding anniversary in the mission station where I was working.'

Penny felt Clive's hands tightening on her arms as they lay together on the hot sand.

'I'm sorry,' she whispered again. Words were inadequate to express her feelings. She was sorry Clive had suffered and she was sorry she'd doubted him. But she still believed he must have dreamed that phone call. Victor wouldn't tell lies. . .would he? But she wasn't going to admit her theory to Clive.

'I suppose if I'd been there when you phoned. . .' she began, but he silenced her with a long, lingering kiss.

When she came up for air he was looking down at her with deeply emotional eyes. 'If Victor hadn't given me that awful message, telling me how you felt about me, I would have insisted you fly out at once to be near me.'

'And you wouldn't have married Sister Jane, would you?'

He gave her a playful smile. 'The whole course of history would have been changed. But let's start the rewrite now. Let's pretend we met yesterday. We looked across a crowded room and I thought you were the most beautiful girl I'd ever seen. So I asked you to have dinner with me and afterwards. . .'

'Afterwards was a romantic dream,' she filled in breathlessly as he pulled her closer into his arms.

His lips were hot and sensual with a hint of the salty sea as they blended with hers. She found herself transported on to a higher plain. Overhead, the seagulls wheeled and cawed as they waited to pounce on the unsuspecting fish that besported themselves in the crystal-clear sea. The water lapped gently on the shore, but otherwise all was silent. There was no indication of the twentieth century. Penny felt as if she were a mythical princess from ancient Egypt being wooed by her king. There was no yesterday, no tomorrow, only the present moment with all the physical and spiritual excitement that their two bodies entwined could produce.

Relieved of all doubts, she gave herself up to the heady excitement of their lovemaking. Clive's embrace became her whole world, and within this sensual enclave she revelled in total abandon. His hands were caressing her warm skin, moving ever more enticingly until she longed for total fulfilment.

And when he entered her she shuddered with an ecstasy that rose higher and higher until, at the final climax of their union, she gave out a long, low moan of exquisite pleasure.

CHAPTER TEN

PENNY'S last day at the clinic on the Red Sea passed in a haze of excitement. She knew she had so much to do before she and Clive could leave for Luxor, but it was difficult to concentrate now that her entire world had been turned upside-down. She thought she'd been in love with Clive the first time, but second time around she was bowled over by her churning emotions.

Their idyllic time on the remote sandy island seemed like a dream and she had to keep on convincing herself that it had actually happened. Now, as she skimmed through the patients' notes, preparing to hand over to the new Egyptian sister, she had to constantly stop as her mind flitted away across the blue sea.

She pushed the notes to one side of the consulting-room desk. Dr Fakry had suggested she work in there while he saw patients in the treatment-room. She hadn't seen Clive that morning. Apparently he was organising the setting up of a new clinic in a nearby hotel. This had been one reason for his journey over from Luxor. That and the fact, as he'd told her last night, that he wanted to escort her back across the desert.

Oh, God. . .she must concentrate! Her replacement sister was due in half an hour and she'd promised Clive she would be ready to leave as early as possible in the afternoon.

But for a couple of minutes she raised her eyes and looked out across the beautiful gardens, bright with hibiscus and bougainvillaea, to the Red Sea. The waves were gently lapping on the shore. . .just as they had done on their island yesterday.

She thought of it now as their island. Because she knew they would return there. . .after they were married. There! She'd allowed herself to daydream the ultimate. Because, although Clive hadn't actually proposed, she thought he'd intimated that their relationship was now permanent.

She leaned back against the chair and felt a slight bruising of her spine. She smiled at the memory of Clive's hard body covering her own, of the ecstasy of their union. . .

She caught her breath at the memory. Deliberately she turned her thoughts away from their passion. The interlude after they'd made love had also been wonderful — swimming together in the warm sea, exploring the underwater world with their masks and snorkels, and admiring the exotic colours of the fish.

And then they'd set out the picnic on a tablecloth on the still warm sand as the sun's rays had begun to slant. Clive had put his shirt around her damp shoulders and she'd revelled in the virile, masculine scent of him.

There had been cold chicken, crusty bread, fruit and a bottle of chilled white wine from the cold container. It had seemed like a feast of the gods.

But before they could start, the boat had returned, speeding around into their little bay, disturbing their tranquil Robinson Crusoe island. The captain had been full of apologies that he and the crew had stayed away longer than the two hours Clive had requested. They had started fishing out on one of the coral reefs and lost all track of time.

'How fortunate for us,' Clive had whispered to her.

'We must have a barbecue,' the captain had shouted to the other two sailors. 'Gather some wood; light a fire; look at this beautiful fish. You never tasted fish like this before. . .'

And the captain had been right. Freshly caught fish, barbecued over a wood fire, seasoned with some kind of sea herb that they'd brought from the depths of the sea made the cold chicken pale by comparison. . .

'Sorry to disturb you, but Sister Khadiga is here. Are you ready to see her?'

Penny looked across the room at Ahmed Fakry standing in the doorway. She had been so many miles away that she hadn't heard his knocking on the door. He remained on the threshold, an amused smile on his lips.

'Are you OK, Penny?' he added quietly. 'You look a bit. . .well — er — sort of spaced-out.'

She smiled. 'I think my brain has taken off for the day. It's difficult to concentrate. But yes, do send Sister Khadiga in. It's time I pulled myself together.'

In an uncharacteristically impulsive movement, the Egyptian doctor crossed the room and leaned over the desk. 'It's good to see you looking so happy, Penny. I'm glad you sorted out your differences. . .whatever they were. Clive looked as if he was—what is your English expression?—walking on cloud nine when I saw him earlier today at the new clinic. Nobody could put a foot wrong. I'm thinking of applying for a salary increase. I expect he'd sign the paper without looking at it.'

Penny laughed. 'Don't you believe it. It takes a lot to put Clive off his stride.'

'Anyway, if congratulations are in order,' Dr Fakry continued, 'I would like to be the first to——'

'Please, Ahmed,' Penny put out her hand towards the Egyptian doctor, 'we also have an old English expression which says, "there's many a slip 'twixt cup and lip". I'd prefer a little caution until. . . until——'

'Sister Byrne. . . I'm Sister Khadiga.'

A small, dark whirlwind of energy had shot into the room and for the next half-hour Penny was totally engrossed in answering the new sister's questions and organising all the medical records.

As she went into lunch she had the secure feeling that she was leaving the clinic in capable hands. It appeared that Sister Khadiga had just come back from a year in the States visiting members of her family who had emigrated there. This was the first job she had applied for since her return and Penny felt they were lucky to have found someone of Sister Khadiga's calibre at such short notice.

Clive didn't appear for lunch. Penny assumed he

must be too busy. She herself wasn't hungry and excused herself after the main course. Her clothes were already packed, but she still had to say goodbye to her in-patients and the rest of the staff.

The sun was low in the afternoon sky when she eventually met up with Clive outside the Red Sea Hotel. The taxi driver was revving his evil-smelling, environmentally unfriendly engine, wishing to make the point that he wanted to get through the desert before nightfall.

'Is this the lot?' Clive picked up her hand luggage to toss it into the boot.

They were the first words they'd spoken to each other since yesterday's protracted goodnight.

'Yes, I think so.'

Their eyes met. The forecourt of the hotel seemed to spin round. The heat that had been building up during the day suddenly felt like a furnace. Penny's cheeks started to burn. Her heart started to pound. Her knees were turning to jelly again. . .and everyone was watching.

It seemed as if the entire staff of the hotel and the clinic had turned out to wave them off. Rumours had been flying around all day about a romance between them, but only Ahmed Fakry had dared to broach the subject. And Penny was glad she'd suggested caution. After all, it was early days. The heady passion of yesterday was a reality, but there was still a long way to go. A relationship between two people was built on more than sensual excitement. She knew that at some point she would have to come down to earth and start being rational.

But for the moment as she climbed into the car beside Clive, she was happy to coast along, to go with her heart. Clive's hand closed over hers as soon as they were out of sight of the hotel.

'Happy?' he whispered.

She snuggled against him. 'Deliriously. And you?'

'Need you ask?' he murmured against her cheek.

She was aware of the driver's eyes reflected in the driving mirror.

'Don't worry about Mahmoud,' Clive whispered. 'He's as reticent as the Sphinx. . .and he only speaks a few words of English. Our secret is safe with him.'

Penny leaned her head back against Clive's arm and wondered why it had to be secret. She wanted to shout it from the rooftops, to let the whole of Hurghada, Luxor, Egypt and the world know that they were in love.

'We've got to call in on Mona, Mohammed's sister and the new baby. Just a routine post examination. I promised Mohammed we'd do it when I saw him this morning.'

'Where did you see Mohammed?'

Clive smiled. 'He came along to the new clinic looking for more work. He knew I was going to be there, of course. I've persuaded the staff to let him work in their newly opened path. lab after school. He'll get more experience there than sweeping floors. He's a very bright boy.

'You really think he'll make it, don't you? Become a doctor, I mean.'

'Oh, it's early days. He certainly has the brain and

the potential, but there's many a slip 'twixt cup and lip.'

Penny felt a cold shiver running down her spine, and she moved away from the crook of Clive's arm to look up at her.

'How strange you should say that. I was only saying the same thing this morning to Ahmed Fakry.'

Clive's blue eyes narrowed. 'Why were you discussing Mohammed with Ahmed?'

'No, no, I simply told him about our English saying that there's many a slip. . . It was a coincidence, that's all,' she finished off lamely.

Clive's eyes were troubled. If he guessed what she'd been discussing with Ahmed he didn't pry any further. And for that she was grateful. Because she wouldn't have known how to explain her subconscious fears, her underlying, inexplicable feeling that all was not well, that this whirlwind romance was too perfect. There had to be a flaw somewhere.

Mona was delighted to see them at her new little house on the outskirts of Hurghada. Her husband was now working as a chef at the nearby hotel and, although money was tight, they were certainly enjoying a higher standard of living than either of their parents. Penny did a lightning tour of the tiny, spotlessly clean, three-roomed, stone-built, one-storey house overlooking the bay of Hurghada and declared she wouldn't mind moving in herself.

Mona beamed. 'Yes, we are very lucky. We buy small piece of land; my husband and his brother work for many weeks and build our house. Then I make curtains and rugs. My father, who is a carpenter, make our bed and the cradle. It's lovely, yes?'

Penny enthused again. It was a simple, idyllic little house that went with this unsophisticated lifestyle. And there was such peace. She found herself wishing that she could banish her own inner turmoil and escape to a tiny house with Clive. To shut out the rest of the world. To have their own babies, live their own lives. . .

But nothing was ever that simple. She and Clive had a long way to go before they could find their own little niche in paradise.

First Clive examined the lusty baby and pronounced him in excellent health. Then Penny assisted Clive when he examined Mona. All the internal organs had fallen back into place and resumed a normal size after the birth. Clive asked if Mona had thought about contraception. It was a routine question which the doctor had to put to all new mothers.

Mona smiled shyly. 'Oh, no. If it is God's will, I will have more babies.'

'How many more do you plan to have?' Clive asked gently.

Mona looked surprised at the question. 'That is not for me to say, Doctor. If God wishes I will have many sons.'

Penny glanced around the tiny room. 'But your house is very small, Mona. Do you think you could cope with a large family?'

The young mother lay back against her pillow, a look of complete serenity on her face. 'God will provide,' she said quietly.

And later, as they drove along the desert road, Penny found herself remembering Mona's serenity. Here was a girl who knew exactly what life was all about.

Why did she find her own life so complicated? What was she waiting for? Would she ever be able to trust Clive implicitly?

His arm around her tightened and she relaxed. She loved him, she adored him. . .but did she trust him? Her eyes closed, lulled by the rocking movement of the ancient taxi.

They stopped in the middle of the desert at a small rest station. An Egyptian served them tea out on the rickety old, paint-peeling wooden veranda. The sun was setting behind the dark, ruggedly hostile mountains and for a moment Penny allowed the full orange glow to bathe her face.

'Penny for them, Penny,' Clvie said, reaching out to take her hand.

She smiled. 'I was thinking what beautiful sunsets there are here in Egypt. It's hard to believe it's almost December. . .nearly Christmas. There'll be no spectacular sunsets for me in England next month.'

She waited for Clive to say something, but he remained silent, watching the last of the sun's rays. Only when the final rusty finger had disappeared did he speak.

'I'd rather hoped you wanted to stay on. . .now.'

She turned and looked at him. His eyes were tender, but gave nothing away. Once more she waited. What was she waiting for? Some kind of commitment, she supposed. She was waiting for him to sweep her into his arms, confess his undying love and beg her never to leave him. Perhaps things like that only happened in films and romantic novels. Maybe in the real world, when the passion died down you just had to take what fate threw at you.

Oh, no! Not this girl! She had her pride. He'd let her down once and it had done nothing for her ego. It was all or nothing from now on. She wasn't a toy to be picked up and put down at whim.

'I'd like to spend Christmas in England,' she said carefully. 'I haven't seen my family for ages and Christmas is the perfect time for a reunion.'

'So you've had enough of travelling?'

'Not necessarily.' Keep your options open, girl!

'The sister you replaced at Luxor has had her baby. She'll be returning just before Christmas.'

'How convenient!'

The last vestige of pink had left the surrounding sand and the inky blackness of the desert night had taken over. A few stars were lending a faint illumination.

'I'd like to go on,' Penny said quietly. 'This place gives me the creeps. How can anyone live out here all alone in the desert?'

Clive laughed. 'We all have to live somewhere. Maybe our host was born out here. Maybe this is the only life he knows. In the final analysis, roots are everything. You're longing to see your family, aren't you?'

'What about you?' she countered.

'Me?' The question seemed totally unexpected.

Clive shrugged. 'I suppose I'm the exception to the rule. I've never felt the need for roots. As the song goes, "Wherever I lay my hat. . ." I'm happy in my profession. It takes me all over the world. I love travelling and——'

'But what about family? Your mother, father, sisters, brothers?' she asked breathlessly.

His face clouded over. 'I had a mother who put me up for adoption as soon as I was born. My adoptive parents died in a car-crash when I was three. I vaguely remember them. Their relatives put me in an orphanage. I suppose you could say I grew up having a large family around me. I always had brothers and sisters to play with. And later, when the authorities found out I was hell-bent on becoming a doctor, I was given a small study where I could do my homework undisturbed.'

Penny's heart was moved. She reached forward and put her hand on Clive's arm. 'What a pity you missed out on real family life.'

Clive gave a slow smile and shook his head. 'Not really. What you've never had you never miss. I didn't think I was missing out. And I achieved my ambition, which was the main thing. I've got a good life now. . .and I can have my own family.'

He reached forward and took her face in his hands, bending his lips to touch hers oh, so lightly and tenderly that she caught her breath.

Was now the time to tell him about the baby she'd lost five years ago. . .his baby? She closed her eyes. How would he react? Would it bring him closer? Would he be sad. . .or relieved?

'Let's go!'

Clive was pulling her to her feet and the moment had passed. One day she would tell him. As soon as she knew they were going to spend the rest of their lives together...and make more babies. Not as many as in her own crowded family, perhaps, but enough to make them into a happy family unit.

She continued to dream as she leaned back against Clive's arm in the back of the taxi. They were speeding along the dark tortuous desert road and she closed her eyes so that she wouldn't worry whether the driver knew the road well enough to go at such tremendous speed. He was anxious to get back to his family, she knew. And she thought of her own family who would give her a tremendous welcome at Christmas, of the smell of the turkey roasting in the oven all through Christmas morning, of her mother poised over the gravy pan, her greying hair damp in the steamy kitchen, a happy smile on her chubby, rosy face as she called out instructions to her daughters.

'Don't leave those sprouts too long, Kitty. Go and fetch your brothers to the table now, Loretta. And make sure they've washed their hands.'

Yes, she would go back. But would she return?

CHAPTER ELEVEN

PENNY was catapulted into work as soon as dawn broke over the Nile. Arriving back late, she and Clive had gone straight to their own rooms in the Nile Hotel to get some rest. She was happy to be in the same spacious, Nile-view room, and the moment her head touched the pillow she fell asleep. But the shrilling of the phone at the same time as the dawn incantation from the minaret across the river on the west bank was less than welcome.

'I need you down in the clinic, stat!' Clive's voice was early morning husky and weary from lack of sleep. 'It's Sarah. . . Sarah Greenwood, you remember, our obstetrics patient. We've kept her as an in-patient on complete bed rest, but I think she's got pre-eclampsia. Staff Nurse Nadia has been staying here at the clinic for the past couple of nights because she was worried about her. She called me down just now and I'm afraid all the cardinal signs of pre-eclampsia are there—hypertension, oedema, proteinuria. . .'

'I'm on my way.'

It took Penny five minutes to throw on her blue and white uniform, scrape her hair under her white cap, and head for the lift.

We'll have to induce, she thought grimly as the lift began its descent. Poor Sarah! After all she's been through to keep this baby, and now this. As far as she could remember without looking at the notes, Sarah must be about thirty-seven weeks by now. Not too early for an induction. The risk of eclampsia, a sometimes fatal condition, if their patient were allowed to continue the pregnancy had always to be balanced against the risk of prematurity. It sounded as if Staff Nurse Nadia had been doing a good job in Penny's absence. She would soon bring her up to date on Sarah's condition.

The lift stopped and Penny ran the few yards around the garden path that led into the clinic. Overhead the exotic birds in their cages were calling to each other in early morning excitement as the orangey-red fingers of the morning stroked the rooftops. The tall wooden mast of a felucca moored on the riverbank was suddenly turned to gold by the first flush of sunlight.

Another beautiful day was dawning. Penny wished she could peer into a crystal ball and see what would be the outcome. There was no doubt that Sarah was in grave danger. In the old days she wouldn't have stood a chance. She would have been just another childbirth casualty. But, thanks to modern technology, they would be able to save mother and baby. . . God willing. Suddenly, her confidence in man-made techniques faltered and she wished she had the unshakeable faith of that young mother over on the Red Sea.

'Thank you for coming down so quickly.' Clive took hold of both her hands and looked down into her eyes. 'We've got to move quickly. Staff Nurse

Nadia has just taken a blood-pressure reading of 160 over 100.'

Penny drew her breath. 'Induction?'

Clive nodded. 'We've no choice. Help me set up the IV.'

As soon as the cannula was *in situ*, Penny started the flow of the drug that would quickly stimulate the uterus into beginning contractions. Clive, meanwhile, had assembled the equipment for an epidural.

'This induction is going to be pretty quick,' he told Penny quietly as he adjusted the IV. 'I don't want Sarah to suffer, so we'll take away the pain with the epidural.'

Clive inserted a local anaesthetic into their patient's epidural space and Sarah appeared more comfortable almost at once. As the below-waist sensory stimuli disappeared she even joked with Penny.

'Can't think what sort of baby I'm going to produce after all this performance. I expect he'll be like his father — histrionic, never doing anything by halves, and utterly self-centred.'

Penny shot her patient a worried glance. 'How is your husband, Sarah?' As she spoke she was remembering the last evening she'd seen the errant James Greenwood escorting a blonde bimbo out of the hotel and into a calèche that headed towards the bright lights of Luxor.

'I don't see much of him. . . He's so busy with his work,' Sarah replied.

Busy, my foot! Penny thought, but now was not the time to disillusion the poor girl.

When the delivery of the foetus was imminent Penny put on her sterile gown and gloves. Staff Nurse Nadia sat beside their patient, holding her hand and instructing her to pant. Penny could see the head emerging. Clive was keeping it flexed in order to prevent tearing of the perineum.

'Check the umbilical cord, Penny.'

Penny reached forward and slid a finger under the patient's pubic arch and, making contact with the umblical cord, she slipped it over the baby's head to prevent undue tightening around its neck during the final part of the delivery.

Clive eased out the tiny, wrinkled shoulders and then, in a matter of seconds, the new baby emerged, pink and bawling, like a child hurtling down an aquatic slide.

'What is it?' Sarah asked, even before the baby had been lifted on to her abdomen.

Clive wrapped the wet bundle in a dressing sheet and handed it to the exhausted mother.

'A girl?' Sarah said in disbelief. 'I was so sure I had a boy. I hope James won't be disappointed.'

Penny swallowed hard. 'Where is your husband?'

'He had to go up to Aswan again. But he'll be back this afternoon. . . Oh, isn't she gorgeous? I'm glad it's a girl, even if James wanted a boy. I suppose I just wanted to please him.'

Penny took the precious bundle from the elated mother. I suppose you did, she thought angrily. Your husband simply doesn't deserve you.

She swabbed the little baby's eyes and removed the mucus from the tiny nostrils, thinking all the time what a darling little baby she was. Many of her new-born infants looked like old people who'd just survived an underwater journey after a deep-sea-diving contest, but this little girl was already beautiful.

'Well worth all the trauma,' Penny said later as she handed the baby to the new mother for her first feed.

'Indeed she is,' Sarah said happily, snuggling up against her new daughter. 'James will love her. Has he contacted you yet, Sister?'

Penny put on her well practised professional smile. 'Not yet, Sarah, but he will.'

She hoped! For all they knew the odious two-timing husband could have taken off for good. Or perhaps he was simply the kind of man who liked to keep his wife chained at home with family commitments while he enjoyed his pseudo-bachelor existence.

The phone rang in the consulting-room towards the end of the morning. Clive had finished seeing patients and Penny was clearing up the debris from a badly bleeding little boy who'd trodden on a broken bottle. It had seemed easier to cleanse, stitch and bind the wound in the consulting-room rather than move the distressed child into any further foreign and disorientating surroundings.

One hand holding a kidney dish of dirty swabs, Penny picked up the phone and recognised James Greenwood's smooth voice.

'How's my wife? I got a message to say she was in a spot of bother. Nothing serious, I hope.'

Penny took a deep breath. 'It might have been, so

we decided to induce the baby. You have a daughter, Mr Greenwood, born at ——'

'A daughter? Are you sure? You've not having me on, are you?'

Penny was trying hard to be patient. 'Well, there was a fifty-fifty chance it would be a girl. Would you like me to give you all the details?'

'No, thanks. I'll only forget them. Sarah can fill me in when I come to see her.'

'When will that be? Your wife has been asking for you.'

'Probably this evening. . .with any luck. . .if I can conclude this little bit of business. But I can't promise anything, mind.'

'Oh, don't put yourself to any inconvenience,' Penny said caustically. 'Your wife is an expert hands and she's not going anywhere today.'

She felt better after she'd slammed the phone down.

'You don't like James Greenwood, do you?' Clive remarked unnecessarily.

'Huh! Does anyone?'

Penny stood up and went to stare out of the window across the hotel gardens. The tourists were gathering beside the pool for lunch snacks. No one was actually swimming in the pool. Although the December sun was hot in the middle of the day the pool remained decidedly chilly. But everyone lay around it, suntan-blocked and somnolent, faces raised to the life-giving heat, and eyes closed behind the latest designer sunglasses.

'I expect Sarah loves him,' Clive replied quietly.

Penny swung round. 'Then she's a fool! She must be blind not to see he's two-timing her.'

'Maybe she knows...or at least suspects...and doesn't want to admit it to herself for fear of losing him. Some women are like that.'

'I'm not!'

Penny surprised herself by the ferocity of her pronouncement. Usually she tried so hard not to get emotionally involved with her patients. But this betrayal had really touched her. And there were parallels in her own life, unpleasantly familiar undertones that stirred up her own misgivings.

Clive got up from the desk and crossed the room to put his hands on her shoulders. Slowly he bent his head, but she remained taut and rigid, moving her head away so that he couldn't kiss her.

'I know you're not like Sarah,' Clive murmured huskily. 'And I'm glad you're a tough, independent, stubborn girl. That's the way I like—dare I say love?—you.'

She closed her eyes and leaned against him, letting her rigid body melt into sensual suppleness.

'There, that's better.' He unpinned her cap and stroked her hair with his hands gently, as if she were a child. 'Now why don't you tell me what's got into you since we left Hurghada? We were all set for the romance of the century and you put up the don't-touch-me sign. What have I done?'

She looked up into his eyes and saw only tenderness. Oh, God, how she loved this man, this raw hunk of masculinity who only had to look at her to turn her knees into jelly.

She took a deep breath. It was now or never. 'You abandoned me when I needed you. I was going to have a baby. . .your baby.'

He gasped. 'Oh, my love! But why didn't you tell me? Why did Victor say you wanted to forget me, never to see me again and——'

'I wanted to tell you. I waited for you to contact me. I was over the moon and——'

'And I would have been over the moon. You've no idea!' He held her against him so hard that she could feel the pounding of his heart.

She pushed aside the stethoscope that was pressing into her and nuzzled her head against his shoulder. She felt so safe in his arms.

'Believe me, Clive, I think you must have dreamt that phone call. Victor wouldn't have concocted a story like that. Why don't you just accept that you were semi-comatosed and——'

'No, I remember it too vividly. I remember so much detail. I've had five years to think about it. But what happened to your baby. . .to our baby?' he asked breathlessly.

She took a deep breath. It seemed like only yesterday. 'I was on duty in the hospital and I needed another gown from the linen cupboard. They were on the top shelf, I remember. I've reached for them hundreds of times, but it was early morning and I think I was a bit faint. . .in fact, now I come to think about it, I was feeling nauseous and longing to go off duty after a long night. I remember pulling the step-ladder towards me and climbing on to it. It wobbled as I reached to top step and I lost my balance. I went crashing down on to the stone floor. I banged my head on something...one of the wooden shelves, I think, because I passed out for a few minutes. Somebody shrieked and it brought me round. There was a sea of faces in the doorway, all staring down at me. I seemed to be lying in a puddle. I thought how strange that the floor was so wet and then I saw that it was blood... Oh, dear, I think I'm going to cry.'

Clive held her against him until the racking sobs had subsided. As she became calm again she realised that was the first time she'd cried so hard. She'd often wanted to grieve for the little one she'd lost. But now, here in the arms of the man who'd started everything, she was able to acknowledge her grief.

'Here, wipe your eyes, my love,' Clive whispered, handing her a freshly laundered linen handkerchief.

'You're so good for me,' Penny said.

'Not as good as I would have been if I'd known how you'd suffered. You should have told me before.'

She rubbed the handkerchief across her face. It smelt of Clive's aftershave. 'I wanted to tell you... so many times...but I had to be sure.'

He looked puzzled. 'Had to be sure of what? Of me? Haven't I made it perfectly clear that I love you ...that I want to spend the rest of my life with you?'

The ground was shifting beneath her feet. She'd heard of the earth moving during lovemaking, but this was ridiculous! The room was spinning and when she tried to speak her voice sounded breathless and far-away.

'You have now.'

He pulled her once more into his arms and kissed her tear-stained cheeks gently at first and then, as their passions rose, he sought her lips.

'I think we'd better take the rest of the day off,' he murmured as they came up for air. 'We can keep in contact with Sarah. Nurse Nadia can stay in the clinic. But I think you and I need a siesta to recover from our late night and early morning labours. . .purely from a medical point of view, you understand.'

Her eyes danced as she smiled up into his eyes. 'But of course. You can be so persuasive, Doctor.'

He laughed. 'I amaze myself at times. Here, put your cap back on and try to look normal for a few minutes so we can set up our afternoon idyll. Your place or mine?'

'Mine,' she said happily. 'I can rest better in my own surroundings.'

'Who said anything about resting?' Clive quipped as he picked up the phone to begin preparations for their romantic interlude.

They had smoked salmon and cucumber sandwiches and a bottle of champagne from Room Service. The boy who delivered the order didn't bat an eyelid when Dr Hamilton strode out of Penny's bathroom in a white mid-thigh-length towelling robe that showed off the excellent tan on his muscular body to perfection.

Clive scribbled his name on the order and

requested no phone calls except from the clinic. Penny, lying in the scented bath, was having hysterics. It didn't seem in the least bit strange that Clive should be taking over her domain. In fact she could get used to being married to him very easily, she thought. As soon as he popped the question she knew what her answer would be.

Their siesta must have lasted a couple of hours. In some ways it seemed like an eternity and in others it was over in a flash. There wasn't enough time to be alone together, to explore each other's bodies, to caress, to probe, to love each other to saturation point.

But at the end of the afternoon, as Penny lay in Clive's arms, her skin drenched in sweat and tingling with heaven-sent sensations, she knew that the physical side of their relationship couldn't be better.

The afternoon had been a revelation. They'd laughed and played together like joyous children and made wild, passionate love like sensual adults. And she had no doubt whatsoever that they were compatible in every way.

'Well, we've had the trial marriage; how about the real thing?' Clive said, leaning across to stroke her cheek.

'Are you proposing, Dr Hamilton?' Penny asked, pulling the sheet up against her naked breasts in mock-shyness.

Clive gave a wry smile. 'I think that's what I'm doing. I've never done it before.'

'How about Sister Jane? Didn't you propose to her?'

Clive's eyes flickered. 'No. It just sort of happened. I'd got involved with her for our own mutual comfort. Actually, I'd got to know her personal physician out in Hong Kong. He told me about the leukaemia just about the time when I was planning to start cooling down our relationship. I didn't like to leave Jane then. But she never knew I stayed on and married her because of rather than in spite of the leukaemia. I felt I owed her something for all the comfort she'd given me after you'd turned me down.'

'I didn't turn you down,' Penny said quietly.

'So you say.'

Penny drew in her breath. It was still there, in spite of everything, this denial of the other's story. She knew she was right and that Clive had imagined the phone call. Clive thought he'd made it and that she was now changing her story.

She leapt out of bed and went over to the window, telling herself it wasn't worth arguing about. Five years was a long time. They'd both changed. They could have a wonderful future together so long as they didn't keep harping on about the past. The past was over. . .finished!

'Let's go for a ride in a felucca,' she cried gaily.

Clive was out of bed in an instant, pulling her against his hot, damp, naked body as they looked out over the Nile.

'We'll ride in a felucca, we'll visit the Valley of the Kings and see the tomb of Tutankhamun, and we'll go to the *son et lumière* at Karnak Temple. But we'll have to get a move on. Only three weeks to Christmas. I'm looking forward to your mother's Christmas dinner.'

Penny swung round, her eyes wide with astonishment. 'Are you planning to go to England too?'

He laughed, and, picking her up in his arms, he swung her up towards the ceiling as if she were a child.

'Put me down, Clive; put me down and answer my question.'

He held her against him to stop the trembling that had taken over her entire body.

'Of course I'm going to England. You don't think I'm going to lose you a second time, do you? And you can surely get me an invitation to your family Christmas. After all, your father will want to vet his future son-in-law.'

'Oh, Clive, I'm so happy.'

His arms were stealing around her again. He was carrying her back to bed.

The phone rang. Sister Nadia sounded worried.

'Sorry to disturb you, Dr Hamilton. Can you come down to see Sarah?'

'We're on our way.'

Clive put the phone back on its cradle.

For an instant Penny allowed herself to luxuriate in the new-found confidence that being accepted as Clive's partner gave her. He wasn't trying to hide their love any more. Like her, he wanted the whole world to know about them.

Nothing could go wrong now. . .could it?

CHAPTER TWELVE

SARAH GREENWOOD was sobbing hysterically when Clive and Penny reached her private room in the clinic. The new-born infant, slumbering in her cot beside the maternal bed, appeared totally oblivious to the unfolding drama.

'James hasn't arrived. Something must have happened to him on the road from Aswan. I just feel it in my bones.'

Clive gave an imperceptible movement of his head that told Penny to take over the counselling. A woman would have more insight in a situation like this, he seemed to be implying.

Penny sank down at the edge of the patient's bed and took hold of Sarah's hand.

'Hush, Sarah. You mustn't upset yourself. I told you that James had said on the phone that he would be here as soon as he'd finished his business. He's a very busy man, you know. He can't —'

'And there's another thing. I know it sounds disloyal of me to talk to you about it, but I think he's been seeing another woman. Last time he came to visit me he was reeking of cheap scent.'

'Perhaps it was some aftershave he'd bought in the market,' Penny said quickly and caught the surreptitious look of approval from Clive who was now, ostensibly, examining the baby's umbilicus and repositioning the bandage.

'Oh, you're only making excuses like the rest of the staff. Nobody believes me. . .but a wife knows about these things. There are tell-tale signs you can't ignore.'

Penny drew in her breath. Her heart was bleeding for this poor woman. What could she say to console her? Should she compound the myth that it was all in her patient's mind or should she be more truthful?

Thankfully, Clive stepped into the breach. Firmly fixing the cotton sheet around the new-born infant, he reached across and took the mother's hand in his.

'Sarah, life isn't always what we'd like it to be. But there are always compensations. You've got your perfect little daughter here. She arrived in this world against tremendous odds and for that we must all be thankful. You've got to balance that against the fact that her father may be less than perfect. Like other young men of his age he may sometimes stray. . .not because he wants to leave you. . .but because it inflates his male ego to——'

Penny clasped a hand over her mouth to stifle the spontaneous gasp as the door was flung open. James Greenwood, standing on the threshold, had caught the last few words of Clive's attempt at soothing their patient, and the thundercloud on his brow was issuing storm warnings.

'I'll thank you to mind your own business, Doctor,' he said with steely calm.

Clive rose to his full height and strode over to the door. 'My business is the welfare of my patients, both mental and physical. The two go together. You can't have a healthy patient who's worry about where her husband is and who he might be dating tonight.'

'That's a slanderous accusation. I've a good mind to call my solicitor.'

'I'm sure you have...but I don't think you will. Do come in, Mr Greenwood. Your wife has been longing to see you. Perhaps you'll come along to see me before you go.'

Clive swept out of the room. Penny also decided it was time to leave the husband and wife alone. There was nothing more they could do. Sarah was rubbing her eyes and looking apprehensive.

Penny patted her hand. 'I'll come back later to settle you down for the night.'

As she walked past the young husband she deliberately avoided looking at him. She closed the door on the pair of them and prayed, as she walked away, that they would effect a reconciliation. At least the outbreak of the matrimonial storm had started to clear the air. It had been brewing for far too long. Sarah was no fool. She must have known all along and tried to sweep it under the carpet, as Clive had surmised. Being ten years older than her husband must make her feel even more vulnerable.

'What a swine!' Penny said as she closed the door behind her in the consulting-room.

Clive looked up from the desk. 'I agree, but we'll have to let them sort it out themselves now. We've delivered the baby and Sarah will soon be fit enough to go back to James. Then we'll have to put them out of our minds and get on with the next medical problem.'

Penny nodded. 'Tough, isn't it?'

Clive got up and came round the side of the desk. 'That's why we need to recharge our batteries so often. I've just booked tickets for tonight's *son et lumière* at the temple of Karnak. Would you like to drive down there in a calèche or a taxi?'

'Oh, need you ask?'

Their calèche drew up outside the hotel promptly at seven-thirty. Staff Nurse Nadia had gone off duty and the competent little Staff Nurse Rania had agreed to hold the fort until they returned. James Greenwood was still ensconced with his wife, sitting beside the bed, holding Sarah's hand, and playing, to all prying eyes, the ideal husband. He had assured Clive that he would still be there on their return from the performance and then they could have their little chat.

Their driver, a rotund, smilingly cheerful Egyptian, his head swathed in a turban and his vast body concealed beneath layers of multi-coloured cotton robes, held out a hand to help Penny into the back seat. Clive climbed in beside her and the horse started off at a good trot through the crowded streets. The moon was providing a good light and the street-lamps and neon signs added their own contribution.

'It's cold,' Penny said in a surprised voice.

Clive wrapped the rug around her knees. 'You haven't been out in the evening in December. It's

Egyptian winter, don't forget. Those few hours of warm sunshine during the day lull you into thinking you're in a tropical country, but Egypt is very much a land of changing seasons.'

'I'm glad I put my layers on tonight,' Penny said. She was wearing tracksuit bottoms under her jeans, and two sweaters — not very glamorous, but it was what Clive had advised. 'I didn't think it would be necessary.'

'You wait till we're walking around in the open-air temple. You'll be perished!'

'Well, thank you!'

'But the music will make up for it.'

'And the company,' she said, revelling in the feel of Clive's fingers tightening over her own.

She glanced sideways and saw the firm, handsome profile of the man who had asked her to marry him. Would their love have still been so exciting if they'd got together five years ago? And, more importantly, would they still be together five years from now?

The clip clop of the horse's hoofs was soothing as she looked around her, entranced by the night-life of the narrow streets. And then they were trotting along the esplanade beside the river, which was studded with the lights of the many boats moored at the bank. Fairy lights were even strung between boats, giving a carnival atmosphere.

Their friendly driver said he would wait outside the temple and take them back to their hotel. They walked into the temple along an impressive avenue of ancient ram-headed sphinxes. The spectacular show started in the great court and continued as they walked through the great hypostyle hall. The music and the lights were impressive and Penny was enthralled by the story that unfolded. The deeply sonorous voice echoed throughout the huge stone monuments, recounting the history of Thebes, which was the old name for Luxor. Penny was fascinated to hear about the lives of the many pharoahs who built the sancturaries, courts, statues and obelisks in honour of Amun, one of the deities of creation and the patron god of Thebes.

The show finished beside the sacred lake, where a grandstand had been erected. Penny marvelled at the beauty of the lights shining on the water as she sat, her legs protected by a rug against the chill Egyptian night, listening to and watching the final spectacle.

Afterwards as they rejoined their calèche she was silent. The sheer excitement of the proceedings had stirred her more than she had expected. It had put things into perspective. For so long she had been worrying about a mere five years of her life. But tonight she'd been exposed to hundreds. . .thousands of years of strife, petty squabblings, love, hate and deception. Life was the same for every generation. You had to go on and enjoy each moment to the full because it was so transient.

Clive's lips brushed her cheek as the horse drew up in front of their hotel.

'Happy?' he whispered.

She nodded, unwilling to speak in case she broke the magic spell. It had been a refreshing experience, spending so much time with Clive. And it would go on. . .and on. . . She was in charge of her destiny now.

James Greenwood was waiting in Clive's consulting-room, sitting in the comfortable armchair that looked out over the illuminated hotel grounds. He gave them his usual perkily confident smile, but his eyes held a troubled expression.

'You wanted to see me, Doctor.'

Clive took a deep breath. 'Would you like some coffee?'

'Thank you.' The man seemed relieved at the friendly tone of Clive's voice.

Penny busied herself with the percolator while remaining aware of the proceedings. As soon as the coffee was ready she handed out three cups and then sat some feet away from James Greenwood, trying to be as objective as possible. This man obviously needed help, and she mustn't lose sight of that. Her patient was a mature woman, after all, and now that Sarah was no longer pregnant she wasn't quite so vulnerable.

'I think you know how we feel about your two-timing, Mr Greenwood,' Clive began.

Penny held her breath. She'd expected Clive to wrap it up a bit. Maybe he was feeling tired. . .or maybe he was simply trying shock tactics.

Whatever it was, it worked.

James Greenwood's confident air vanished as he put his head in his hands. Penny couldn't see his eyes, but his shaking shoulders indicated that he was weeping. She looked across at Clive, but he seemed prepared to let James take his time. The dam had finally broken open and it would be unwise to try to stem the flow.

It was several minutes before James Greenwood lifted his head from his hands and, red-eyed, looked around at Clive and Penny.

'I've been such a fool. I'd no idea Sarah knew I was playing around and I never thought it would affect her so badly. I would never do anything that would hurt her. You may not believe this, but I do love my wife.'

'Oh, we believe you,' Clive said quietly. 'But your wife was beginning to doubt it when you spent so little time with her. She's a few years older than you and this makes her even more scared she'll lose you. And you've got your daughter to think about now.'

James Greenwood stood up and began to pace the room. 'Don't preach, Doc; for heaven's sake, don't preach. I've decided what I'm going to do. I'm going to get the firm to transfer me back to England, buy a house near my family and settle down. Because if I lost Sarah——'

'And you will lose her,' Penny put in firmly. 'No wife is prepared to put up with playing second fiddle. She wants to be your number one and you'd better make sure she is. Because if you lose her, you'll lose custody of your little daughter and——'

'Don't! I know. We've argued it all out this evening and I've promised never to look at another woman again.'

There was silence in the room for a few minutes. Penny sipped her coffee and felt a warm glow of happiness stealing over her. Maybe this wandering husband had seen the light just in time.

James Greenwood stood up. 'I never thought I would say this to you, Doctor, but thanks for everything...and I mean everything. I must admit I thought the pair of you were a couple of busybodies, but you've probably saved our marriage. When will Sarah be fit to leave here?'

'She's probably better in the clinic until you go back to England. The baby is three weeks premature so she's going to need special care for a few weeks. How soon before you can effect a transfer?' Clive asked.

'I'll get on to it first thing tomorrow morning. My MD owes me a favour. He's not going to be pleased when I say I want to quit travelling, but he'll get used to it... I hope! Anyway, my marriage is the most important thing in my life now.'

Clive and James Greenwood shook hands before he left.

Penny looked at Clive as the door closed. 'Do you think he'll stick it out? In other words, can a leopard change his spots?'

Clive smiled. 'Only time will tell. All I can say at the moment is that he's full of good intentions. I think he's started to look at Sarah in a different light. She's made it clear she's not going to put up with his philandering, so he's had to make a choice.'

'And not before time!' Penny said vehemently. She stifled a yawn with the back of her hand. 'I'm going to turn in. For some unknown reason I feel absolutely whacked.'

Clive smiled. 'You've had an exhausting day, Sister. Run along and get your beauty sleep. I'm going to catch up on some paperwork while it's quiet. I'm setting up another clinic about half a mile away and there's a lot of organisation still to do. Tomorrow I'm interviewing staff there. This is one of the projects I had to work on while you were over on the Red Sea. ICMWT is expanding all the time.'

'So will you be coming back to Egypt after Christmas?'

Clive shrugged. 'I expect so. But then in my contract I agreed to go wherever I was needed most. So I shall just have to wait and see.'

'So you've never considered going back to live in England permanently?'

Clive shook his head. 'Never enters my mind. I love travelling. I enjoy the challenge of new medical situations, sorting out staffing problems, effecting a variety of cures, surgery under difficult conditions. . .' He paused and smiled down at her. 'It would be difficult to make me change my career. . . even for a woman.'

Penny drew in her breath. 'Are you trying to tell me something?'

'Only that I hope you like travelling. I know you're adaptable, unflappable and resourceful. You didn't expect we would settle down in suburban boredom, did you?'

Her spirits rose. 'I wasn't sure whether your travel plans included me. I thought maybe I was going to be the little woman stoking the fires while her husband swanned off to foreign parts.'

He pulled her close. 'Of course you're included. It takes a special sort of wife to put up with my lifestyle and that's why I know you'll be perfect. Now go and get some sleep.'

CHAPTER THIRTEEN

THERE was only a week before Clive and Penny were due to leave for their Christmas in England. They were still extremely busy at the clinic, but Clive insisted that they must finish off in style by sampling some of the tourist attractions.

He arranged to take Penny out in a felucca one afternoon after surgery. They took a picnic with them and, after the brief sail over the water, settled themselves on Banana Island, a small, picturesque, sandy, palm-tree-bedecked strip of land in the middle of the Nile. The two Egyptian sailors who had brought them to the island remained in the felucca, mending one of the sails that had torn in the high wind.

Even in the middle of the day with the hot sun shining down on them it was definitely feeling colder.

'The weather is preparing us for England,' Penny said with a smile as she bit into a piece of melon at the end of their picnic.

Clive agreed. 'Have you warned your parents I'm coming with you?'

'I don't think "warn" is quite the right word, Clive. I've phoned them a couple of times and they're delighted. They can't wait to meet you. I've insisted we stay at the nearby hotel, though. Our house is bursting at the seams as it is.'

Clive didn't look up from his task of clearing the debris back into the wicker basket. 'And I've booked the tickets. Give me the name of the hotel and I'll phone for a reservation for us.'

'I've already done it.'

Clive looked up and gave her a wry smile. 'One room or two?'

She hesitated. 'Two. . .just in case.'

He frowned. 'Just in case of what?'

'Just in case you snore,' she ad-libbed lightly. 'And in case my mother should drop in uninvited. My parents aren't exactly enlightened. . . I mean they're totally old-fashioned in their ideas about what couples should do before marriage.'

She looked across the brown swirling water of the Nile. It was really happening at last. Her wish was coming true. She felt almost certain that nothing could spoil the dream. Why was there that tiny doubt in her mind? What was still troubling her?

The past was still there. . .but she mustn't think about it, mustn't allow it to spoil her happiness.

Clive reached across and folded her into his arms. 'I wish I knew what was going on in your head when you get that far-away look. The sooner I make an honest woman of you the better.'

His kiss was tender, the kiss of a well practised lover who was beginning to understand the whims and delights of his mistress. Penny closed her eyes and savoured the moment.

How many more moments? said the tiny doubting voice from the depths of her subconscious.

Forever, whispered her heart.

How can you be so sure? said the rational voice.

On another day, as part of their personal tourist education campaign, Clive had arranged for one of the doctors from the hospital to come in and relieve him. Penny's place was taken by the two staff nurses, Nadia and Rania. Early in the morning Clive and Penny took a boat across to the west bank and hired a taxi to drive them to the Valley of the Kings.

Penny had an immense feeling of awe as they were driven up the steep, dusty road into the canyon of the tombs where the mighty kings had once lain in great stone sarcophagi awaiting immortality. They visited all the main tombs, marvelling at the ancient decorations and pictures that had survived intact over the centuries. It seemed incredible that the colours should have remained vivid throughout the years.

They spent time in each tomb they visited, emerging into the bright sunlight with a feeling of unreality that they should be plunged back into the twentieth century. It was almost noon and a crowd had gathered outside the entrance to the tomb of Tutankhamun. A guide at the entrance informed them that they would have to wait until the people already inside emerged to make space for more visitors.

It was no hardship to stretch out on a warm stone slab in the noonday sun and look up at the blue sky flecked with tiny white clouds.

One week to Christmas, Penny thought. It wasn't her usual run-up to the festive period. She hadn't done any shopping, written any cards, or helped her mother stir the puddings and the cake. But nothing was usual any more. Normality had receded as she'd given herself up to this wonderful romance.

She turned on her side to look at Clive and saw that he was intently watching a group of young English boys who were running around the hillside as they waited their turn to go and inspect the tomb.

'Presumably someone is in charge of those boys,' he said, shielding his eyes from the sun as he looked around the area.

A couple of harassed teachers were attempting to control a rowdy group at the entrance to the tomb.

'I think they've overlooked those three up there,' Penny said. 'Maybe we should round them up.'

Even as she spoke there was a loud howl of pain. One of the boys, chased by another, had slipped on the treacherous stony surface, setting off a mini-landslide. He screamed again as he hurtled down the hillside towards the waiting tourists. Within seconds the boy had crashed into a boulder and was now lying inert. The howling had stopped. His two companions were picking their way gingerly down the hillside towards their injured friend.

Clive leapt to his feet and hurried across the slope, Penny making her way behind him as quickly as she dared. it was immediately obvious that the young boy was in pain, and it didn't take long to diagnose the problem. The boy's right leg had taken the full force of his impact with the rock; the tibia had fractured and was plainly visible through the ruptured skin.

Penny took the boy's head in her hands while Clive attempted to stem the flow of blood from the wound. One of the teachers, a young woman, white-faced and shaking, had arrived on the scene.

'Johnny, you were told to stay with the group——' she began, but Clive cut her short.

'I'm a doctor. Go down to the cafeteria and see if you can get some first-aid equipment. They must have some provision for accidents. The boy mustn't be moved except by stretcher or an improvisation of that nature. A few planks or a door would be adequate.'

The staff in the cafeteria were extremely helpful, bringing out blankets and a stretcher as soon as they were alerted. Penny and Clive supervised the lifting of the boy and offered to take him back to the east bank so that the teachers could continue their expedition with the rest of the group.

But the other boys had lost all interest in ancient history and wanted to see their friend safely into hospital. So it was a very large group of boys and teachers who crowded into the casualty department of the hospital when they returned to the east bank.

Clive had been able to administer some morphine to their patient from the first-aid box given to them by the captain of the ship that took them back across the Nile. The boy thankfully dropped into a state of semi-consciousness in which he remained for the rest of the journey.

It was a couple of hours before Clive and Penny

felt they could leave young Johnny in the capable hands of the hospital staff. The boy had come to rely on them during the first part of his ordeal and was unwilling to see them go. But Clive explained that they had their own patients to deal with.

They left him, promising to return the next day.

'I would have admitted him to our clinic if we hadn't been about to leave for England,' Clive said. 'But he needs continuity of care at the moment. And the surgery he's going to require with that fractured tibia is difficult. They've got a good orthopaedic team at the hospital. Initially they'll put him in a long leg plaster until the full extent of the damage can be assessed. He may even be taken back to England for the rest of his treatment. He could travel by air in a long leg plaster. That's what I would do if I were in charge of the case. Because he's only thirteen, still at the age when he needs his mum.'

The day of their departure had arrived. Penny was surprised how sad she was feeling to be leaving Luxor.

'But we shall be coming back in the New Year. Nothing has changed,' Clive said as he snapped the lock on Penny's suitcase.

Penny looked out across the Nile. She would miss her luxurious hotel room and the delights of room service. She would miss the warm midday sun. But Clive was going to be with her for a full two weeks.

'When we get back, I'm going to need you to work

between the two clinics,' Clive was saying. 'Have you got your passport handy?'

She nodded. It all seemed so unreal. Was she really taking Clive home to meet the family? And what would they think of him...and what would he make of them?

Hours later, it seemed, they boarded the plane after saying goodbye to the hotel staff, to their patients and to the clinic staff. The hospital had loaned the clinic a couple of doctors for the two weeks they would be away, and Clive had appointed two new Egyptian sisters. Sarah Greenwood had clung to Penny and Clive, thanking them for all their help. There were tears in her eyes as they closed the door of her room, but Penny was sure they were tears of happiness, because she'd seen the new rapport that was building up between Sarah and her husband.

In the sea of smiling faces at the airport had been their young patient Johnny, who, in spite of continuing pain, had taken Clive's advice and requested a transfer to England. Clive and Penny had been able to supervise the loading of their young patient, now encased in a full leg plaster. Four seats had been removed to fix a stretcher bed at the back of the plane, and Johnny was surrounded by his mates, who kept him amused throughout the journey and wrote schoolboy messages on his virgin white plaster.

They touched down at Gatwick airport in the middle of a snowstorm.

'A white Christmas!' Penny breathed, but her

hopes shattered as she saw the flakes turn to soggy puddles on the grimy tarmac.

'Two days to go; it could be possible,' Clive said, putting an arm around her as they walked through the chill corridor towards the baggage reclaim.

Clive had insisted they spend their first night in London, even though Penny had explained that she would have to cancel the hotel rooms in Liverpool.

'For old times' sake,' he'd whispered, and she'd felt the excitement rising inside her.

They waved goodbye to Johnny as he was being loaded into an ambulance. He waved cheerfully back, seemingly none the worse for his journey. And then they were being driven towards London.

Penny held her breath as their taxi drove through Knightsbridge. Trust Clive to be the eternal romantic! The taxi slowed to a halt in front of their hotel.

It was *their* hotel, because this was where it had all started five years ago. She moved as if in a dream through the foyer; nothing had changed. She felt like a young girl again as the lift sped up towards the second floor. And it was the same room, probably the same bed. She couldn't remember it except that it had been wide and wonderfully comfortable, the biggest bed she'd ever seen in all her twenty years.

Clive put out the 'Do not disturb' sign and they undressed as soon as the porter had disappeared. Five years rolled away as they clung to each other, unable to hold back their lovemaking.

And afterwards, as they lay in each other's arms, Penny looked at the dark London sky and saw the flakes of snow thickening.

'It's going to be a wonderful Christmas,' she whispered.

'I've got something to tell you.' Clive was leaning up on one arm, looking down at her, his eyes dreamy with satiated passion. 'You were quite right about that phone call. I couldn't have made it. I was in a deep coma for ages. I guess I dreamed the whole thing.'

She sat up, wide awake, and stared at him.

'Oh, Clive, if only you'd said that before,' she began and then stopped, her eyes narrowing as she watched the impossible man beside her. 'If only you'd realised how much it meant to me to know that. I knew that Victor couldn't have lied. He's such a good man, so reliable.'

Clive's eyes flickered. 'That's what I figured. And I knew it meant so much to you to get the mystery cleared up. . .so there's the first of my Christmas presents.'

'Oh, thank you. It's the best Christmas present I. . .'

She stopped. There was something false about his confession, something that didn't ring quite true. Why was he suddenly admitting, without reservation, that he'd been wrong? And why did he call it a Christmas present? A present was something you gave to someone else.

She leaned back on her pillows and stared up at the ceiling. He was giving her peace of mind for Christmas. That was it! He'd decided it meant so much to her. He'd seen through the silent pauses when she'd regarded him thoughtfully, longing for him to remember what had really happened.

'You're lying,' she said softly. 'You're trying to placate me, aren't you?'

He lay back on the pillows beside her, but removed the arm that had idly encircled her shoulders. She heard the sharp intake of his breath as he spoke sombrely.

'I'm at my wits' end, Penny. I don't know how to convince you of the truth. I thought you'd swallow my explanation just now and that would be the end of it, but obviously I'm a rotten liar. But I'm very good at remembering the truth. It's all so vivid in my mind—Sister Jane dialling the number, handing me the phone; then Victor's voice. I had to strain to hear what he was saying, I remember. There was a terrible racket going on in the background. I asked him if he could speak up and he said that was the loudest he could get because the woman upstairs was having a new kitchen put in and——'

'What did you say?' Penny shrieked.

Clive looked puzzled. 'Victor couldn't shout any louder.'

'No, the bit about the woman upstairs and her kitchen. That's it! You couldn't have known that. I remember the exact timing. Oh, Clive. It was such a deafening racket every day. I was glad to be going on duty. And it was during the time that Victor had to sleep on my sitting-room sofa because he'd run out of rent money.'

'You mean you really believe me now?' Clive gave an exasperated sigh. 'After all you've put me through! I just don't understand how your mind works.' Suddenly, his voice became steely hard. 'But what about Victor, this so-called paragon of virtue? Where does that leave him?'

'In the soup!' Penny replied grimly as she reached for the phone and dialled an outside number.

The practice nurse at Victor's father's surgery, who was an old school friend of Penny's, helpfully informed her that Victor had gone away for Christmas and not left an address. June Grainger thought Victor had gone in seach of some sun.

'But just a minute, Penny,' the nurse said hastily as Penny was about to ring off. 'I've got a letter here to post to you. Victor said he'd missed the last posting dates so would I nip it round to your house as soon as I had a spare minute.'

Penny took a deep breath. 'June, be an angel and open it, will you?'

'Well, if you're sure. . .'

Penny held her breath as she heard the sound of paper being split open. She didn't care what her old school chum thought. She couldn't wait until Christmas Day.

'Well, Victor says,

> "Dear Penny,
> Sorry I won't see you at Christmas. Just heard that you're bringing your intended home to meet the family. So it really was a love match after all! I didn't believe it when I heard. Having always had your best interests at heart ever since you were my favourite playmate, I naturally kept up the guardian angel service when we were in London. I see now that this was a mistake. As

you've probably gathered by now, I improvised when Clive rang up, in an effort to end what seemed at the time to be an undesirable liaison, and when the letter came I filed it in the rubbish bin before you came back off duty.

I knew Clive was working out in Egypt when I suggested you take that job. I hoped the reality would kill the myth. I was wrong again.

Sorry if I've caused you any inconvenience. Obviously it didn't deter the path of true love.

Yours,
Victor."'

Penny forgot that June Grainger was still at the other end of the line as she attempted to digest the information.

'Obviously the path of true love,' she muttered under her breath.

'Are you still there, Penny?' came the embarrassed voice down the phone.

'June, thanks a million. I'll pick the letter up from the surgery some time. Hang on to it. . . Yes, I hope to see you over Christmas. . . We'll be coming up to Mum's. . .'

She put the phone back on the cradle and turned back to look at the man she loved unreservedly. The skeletons were all out of the closet and they were free to get on with their life together.

'I love you, Clive,' she whispered. 'We've wasted so much time. . .'

But his kiss silenced her.

CHAPTER FOURTEEN

THE church was packed. The last of the Christmas decorations had been removed, to be replaced by masses of spring flowers flown in specially for the wedding from the Channel Islands. Penny's mum had spent a whole day, aided and hindered by Kitty and Loretta, turning the church into a miniature flower festival.

Now, as Penny walked slowly down the aisle, she clasped her father's arm firmly to give him strength. She could fee him shaking with nerves, but she felt strong and exhilarated at the thought of the new life ahead. It had been such a rush to fix the wedding so quickly — the special licence, the church, the choir, Father O'Brien delaying his new year holiday to the Emerald Isle so that he could perform the ceremony for one of the favourite members of his flock.

She looked around at the sea of familiar faces and smiled through her long white veil. A traditional wedding — that was what her mother had wanted. . . and had insisted on! Clive would have been happy with a register office ceremony, but wild horses wouldn't deter the bride's mother. No corners were ever cut in the Byrne household.

The taffeta underskirt beneath the sculptured silk gown that her mother had worn rustled as Penny moved on, slowly, whispering to her father to relax.

He gave her a pale imitation of a smile. She knew he would have preferred Clive's original suggestion. He got on well with his son-in-law. It was amazing, the rapport that had sprung up between the two men over Christmas. Penny was sure that the pair of them had celebrated too heartily the night before and that her father's hangover was compounding his nerves.

But Clive looked fit and healthy when she reached the altar. He turned to smile at her and for one moment she thought he was going to take her in his arms.

But that would be later. . .much later, when they had escaped all the razzmatazz of the reception, and were on their way to catch the plane back to Egypt. The honeymoon was to be delayed for a few weeks until full staffing arrangements had been made; then they were going to take off for an unknown destination. . .no phones, no responsibilities, just the two of them.

Clive had said that this was when they would have the fun of trying to start their family. Giving Penny the benefit of his superior medical knowledge, he'd warned her that she might have problems conceiving after the trauma of her miscarriage.

She smiled to herself now as she looked up into his grey eyes and thought of the little secret she was snuggling against her heart. Two days ago she'd been to the chemist and brought home the small package that enabled her to do a pregnancy testing.

Positive! She remembered the glow of excitement. But she hadn't wanted to divulge the secret with the whole family around. She would tell Clive on the plane back to Egypt, when they were alone.

He would be so thrilled!

'Penelope Mary, will you have this man. . .?'

Oh, yes, she would! For richer, for poorer, for anything that life might throw at her. She was totally secure now in her love and nothing could change that.

They were walking back down the aisle. Dr and Mrs Hamilton. It sounded so formal. But they were still Clive and Penny. She felt Clive's fingers tightening on her own. With her veil thrown back she could recognise all her old school friends smiling and giving her their best wishes for the future. And her brothers, wedding-smart and spruced up as she'd never seen them before. And her gran, in a cream woollen suit, leaning forward to kiss the bride and wish her luck.

'Luck doesn't enter into it,' she whispered to Clive as they went out into the pale January sunlight. 'The problems are all behind us now.'

'Except the little ones,' Clive said with a wry grin.

'Funny you should mention it,' Penny replied, giving him a knowing smile.

'Darling! You're not. . .?'

MILLS & BOON

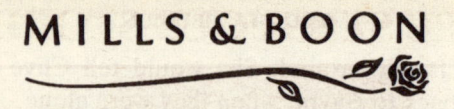

NEW LOOK MEDICAL ROMANCES

To make our medical series even more special we've created a whole new design which perfectly blends heart-warming romance with practical medicine.

And to capture the essence of the series we've given it a new name, chosen by you, our readers, in a recent survey.

Four romances with a medical theme from vets to general practitioners. Watch out for ...

LOVE ON CALL

From October 1993   Price £1.80

Available from W.H. Smith, John Menzies, Martins, Forbuoys, most supermarkets and other paperback stockists.
Also available from Mills & Boon Reader Service, Freepost, PO Box 236, Thornton Road, Croydon, Surrey CR9 9EL. (UK Postage & Packing free)

THREE SENSUOUS STORIES...

Charlotte Lamb
A COLLECTION

THE SEX WAR
DESPERATION
OUT OF CONTROL

A special collection of three bestselling novels from one of the world's foremost romance authors

ONE BEAUTIFUL VOLUME

A special collection of three individual love stories, beautifully presented in one absorbing volume.

One of the world's most popular romance authors, Charlotte Lamb has written over 90 novels, including the bestselling *Barbary Wharf* six part mini-series. This unique edition features three of her earlier titles, together for the first time in one collectable volume.

AVAILABLE FROM SEPTEMBER 1993   PRICED £4.99

W RLDWIDE

*Available from W. H. Smith, John Menzies, Martins, Forbuoys, most supermarkets and other paperback stockists.
Also available from Worldwide Reader Service, FREEPOST, PO Box 236, Thornton Road, Croydon, Surrey CR9 9EL. (UK Postage & Packing free)*

TORN BETWEEN TWO WORLDS...

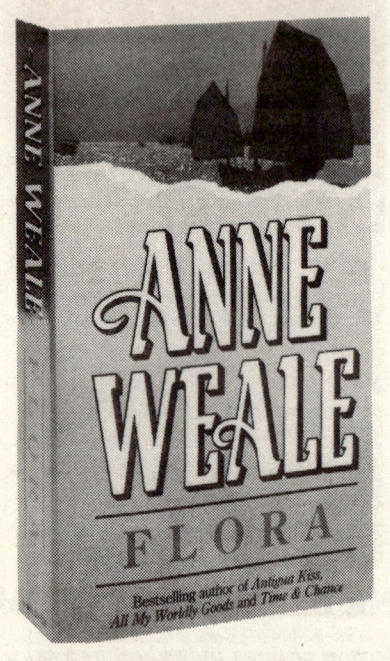

A delicate Eurasian beauty who moved between two worlds, but was shunned by both. An innocent whose unawakened fires could be ignited by only one man. This sensuous tale sweeps from remotest China to the decadence of old Shanghai, reaching its heart-stirring conclusion in the opulent Longwarden mansion and lush estates of Edwardian England.

Available now priced £3.99

WORLDWIDE

*Available from W. H. Smith, John Menzies, Martins, Forbuoys, most supermarkets and other paperback stockists.
Also available from Worldwide Reader Service, FREEPOST, PO Box 236, Thornton Road, Croydon, Surrey CR9 9EL. (UK Postage & Packing free)*

4 MEDICAL ROMANCES AND 2 FREE GIFTS

FROM MILLS & BOON

Capture all the drama and emotion of a hectic medical world when you accept 4 Medical Romances PLUS a cuddly teddy bear and a mystery gift - absolutely FREE and without obligation. And, if you choose, go on to enjoy 4 exciting Medical Romances every month for only £1.70 each! Be sure to return the coupon below today to: **Mills & Boon Reader Service, FREEPOST, PO Box 236, Croydon, Surrey CR9 9EL.**

NO STAMP REQUIRED

YES! Please rush me 4 FREE Medical Romances and 2 FREE gifts! Please also reserve me a Reader Service subscription, which means I can look forward to receiving 4 brand new Medical Romances for only £6.80 every month, postage and packing FREE. If I choose not to subscribe, I shall write to you within 10 days and still keep my FREE books and gifts. I may cancel or suspend my subscription at any time. I am over 18 years.
Please write in BLOCK CAPITALS.

Ms/Mrs/Miss/Mr _____ **EP53D**

Address _____

_____

Postcode _____ Signature _____

Offer closes 31st October 1993. The right is reserved to refuse an application and change the terms of this offer. One application per household. Overseas readers please write for details. Southern Africa write to B.S.I. Ltd., Box 41654, Craighall, Transvaal 2024. You may be mailed with offers from other reputable companies as a result of this application. Please tick box if you would prefer not to receive such offers ☐

mps MAILING PREFERENCE SERVICE

Mills & Boon

MEDICAL ROMANCE

The books for enjoyment this month are:

RED SEA REUNION Margaret Barker
HEART ON HOLD Lynne Collins
HEART CALL Lilian Darcy
A DOUBLE DOSE Drusilla Douglas

♥ ♥ ♥ ♥ ♥

Treats in store!

Watch next month for the following absorbing stories:

THE SPICE OF LIFE Caroline Anderson
A DANGEROUS DIAGNOSIS Jean Evan
HEARTS IN HIDING Alice Grey
LOVE IN A MIST Clare Lavenham

Available from W.H. Smith, John Menzies, Martins, Forbuoys, most supermarkets and other paperback stockists.

Also available from Mills & Boon Reader Service, Freepost, P.O. Box 236, Thornton Road, Croydon, Surrey CR9 9EL.

Readers in South Africa - write to:
Book Services International Ltd, P.O. Box 41654, Craighall, Transvaal 2024.